The Amazing
Panda
Adventure

The Amazing Panda Adventure

A novelization by A. L. Singer
Based on the
Screenplay by Jeff Rothberg and Laurice Elehwany
Story by John Wilcox & Steven Alldredge

SCHOLASTIC INC.
New York Toronto London Auckland Sydney

WARNER BROS. PRESENTS
A LEE RICH/GARY FOSTER PRODUCTION A CHRISTOPHER CAIN FILM "THE AMAZING PANDA ADVENTURE"
STEPHEN LANG YI DING RYAN SLATER MUSIC BY WILLIAM ROSS EXECUTIVE PRODUCER GABRIELLA MARTINELLI
STORY BY JOHN WILCOX & STEVEN ALLDREDGE SCREENPLAY BY JEFF ROTHBERG AND LAURICE ELEHWANY
PRODUCED BY LEE RICH, JOHN WILCOX, GARY FOSTER AND DYLAN SELLERS
DIRECTED BY CHRISTOPHER CAIN

ISBN 0-590-55206-6

12 11 10 9 8 7 6 5 4 3 2 1   5 6 7 8 9/9 0/0

Printed in the U.S.A.   01

First Scholastic printing, August 1995

The Amazing Panda Adventure

Prologue

In the forests of the Szechwan Province, China, a panda cries out.

Less than a half-mile away, another panda is chewing on a bamboo stalk. She hears the cry. Rearing back her head, she lets out a loud, sharp cry of her own. In sympathy.

A golden monkey in a nearby tree hears her. He screeches, swinging toward his family and friends. They, too, pick up the cry.

Soon the entire forest seems to be screaming.

The screams reach a cluster of cages, surrounded by a compound of small build-

ings in Wolong, China. In each cage, a captive panda answers the mad distant cry.

Then, without warning, the noise stops. Deep in the forest, the panda who cried out first has fallen silent. She is lying on her back. Almost lifeless.

Despite her exhaustion, she has enough energy for what is needed.

With a gentle, protective sweep of her arm, she draws her newborn cub to her chest.

In the silence, she hugs him. He looks out, wide-eyed, into his new, unfamiliar home.

Chapter 1

Warm sweat prickled Ryan Tyler's forehead. He took a deep breath.

The time had arrived. His moment of humiliation. His nightmare of horror, on this, the most dreaded day of the seventh-grade school year.

Fathers' Career Day.

Ryan glanced quickly toward the back of the classroom. There they were. The dads. Looking hunched and overgrown in the too-small chairs. All of them smiling proudly.

Lawyers, doctors, fruit vendors, sanitation workers — it didn't matter what they did. Today, everyone's dad had the chance to be a star.

Except Ryan's, that is. Dr. Tyler couldn't be there. He was busy saving pandas in China.

"Ryan?" called Mrs. Grant, his teacher. "Would you like to make a presentation on behalf of your father?"

Ryan's eyes darted toward the door. As if his dad would magically appear. As if Dr. Michael Tyler would fly around the world for an afternoon. Just for Ryan.

Fat chance.

With a sigh, Ryan walked to the front of the class. He cleared his throat and carefully unfolded his speech.

"The giant panda is the most famous animal in the world," he began. "It is the international symbol for peace. Only there's no peace in its life."

Someone yawned. Out of the corner of his eye, Ryan spotted a classmate beginning to doze off.

Great. Not only was his dad thousands of miles away — not only did Ryan have to pinch-hit for him on Career Day — but his great, important job was putting half the class to sleep!

"The pandas live in the forests of China," Ryan barged on, "and because the forests

4

are disappearing, so is the panda. Today there are fewer than one thousand pandas left in the world. But the panda's biggest threat to extinction is that people just don't care. And that's what my father does for a living — he's in China, fighting off lions and tigers and poachers to save the pandas. Just like Indiana Jones."

Three kids rolled their eyes.

Okay, it was an exaggeration. Ryan knew that. But what was he supposed to do, tell the truth? That his dad was a quiet dude with a ponytail who worked on a reserve, trying to get captive pandas to mate? That the only danger he faced was tracking pandas in the forest?

Indiana Jones sounded much better.

"Anyway, that's why he's not here," Ryan continued. "Because saving pandas is more important."

"Thank you, Ryan, that was very nice," said Mrs. Grant, smiling patiently. "And now Johnny Pratt's father will speak about his chosen profession."

Ryan couldn't help noticing Johnny's face. He was beaming. Usually Johnny didn't look that happy unless he was eating junk food.

His belly straining over his belt, Mr. Pratt lumbered toward the front of the class. Everyone watched him, wide-eyed and admiring.

They sat there in rapt silence as he told about the night shift at the 7-Eleven.

That afternoon, Johnny and Ryan left school together. As they walked out to the bus, Ryan was trying hard to erase the day from his memory.

Not with Johnny around.

"The best part of my dad's job," Johnny explained, chomping on a Ding Dong, "is when he brings home Twinkies and other stuff when they pass the expiration date."

"Aren't you worried that they're spoiled?" Ryan asked.

"Pop says that there's enough chemicals in them to choke a moose." With his shirt-sleeve, Johnny wiped flecks of chocolate off his mouth. "But I guess that's nothing compared to saving panda bears."

Ryan shrugged. "Ah, panda bears aren't such a big deal."

As Johnny popped the rest of the Ding Dong into his mouth, he glanced over Ryan's shoulder. "Hey, dude, look out," he warned. "Lucy Sanders is heading right toward you."

Out of the corner of his eye, Ryan could see a flash of golden hair, a gentle swaying of fabric. He needed to see no more. His body was an instant mishmash of emotions — pounding blood, churning stomach.

Lucy Sanders was, in a word, astounding. No girl in the whole school came close.

She had never talked to Ryan. She had never, in Ryan's memory, even looked at him. But now she was approaching, and that meant one thing.

Red alert.

Hair. Ryan hadn't touched it since gym class. He quickly lifted off his Chicago Cubs baseball cap and smoothed the mess underneath.

Clothes. Ryan stuffed his flapping shirttail into his pants.

"How do I look?" he asked Johnny.

Johnny winced. "I don't know. It's not cool to check out other guys."

"Come *on!*"

"All right, your hair's sticking up." Johnny spat into his hand, releasing a globule of saliva and moistened crumbs. With it, he patted down Ryan's flyaway hair. "Go over and meet her."

Ryan froze.

"Go on," Johnny urged.

Ryan stepped toward her. His feet felt like pontoons. His knees began to quiver.

Lucy was turning. *Turning* — toward him! This could be it. The meeting. The start of a beautiful future.

He didn't notice his untied shoelaces until he stepped on them. But by that time, the sidewalk was racing toward his face.

He landed with a dull thud.

Lucy turned away. From his vantage point on the pavement, Ryan had a terrific view of her heels.

Johnny bounded over. "She'll come around," he remarked confidently, helping Ryan to his feet.

Right, Ryan thought. *Girls just go crazy over guys like me. Friendly. Down-to-earth.*

Totally chicken.

Ryan stepped glumly off the bus in front of his house. Johnny tagged along behind him, working on a candy bar.

"Ask your mom if I can stay for dinner,"

Johnny mumbled, his mouth full of chocolate caramel.

"You stay every night," Ryan replied.

"Yeah, but I don't want her thinking I'm a mooch."

Ryan rolled his eyes. "Okay."

Walking onto the front porch, Ryan reached into his mailbox and pulled out a fistful of letters. He eagerly shuffled through them and smiled.

Turning to Johnny, he held up an envelope with a panda face stamped on its upper left corner.

"What's that?" Johnny asked.

"That's the symbol of the reserve where my dad works!"

"Cool."

Clutching the letter, Ryan bolted inside. He dropped the rest of the mail on the coffee table without stopping.

"Hi, sweetheart!" his mom called out from the kitchen.

Ryan whizzed past her and up the stairs. "Hi!"

Huffing and puffing, Johnny followed behind. As he reached the bottom of the staircase, Mrs. Tyler called out, "Johnny, don't get chocolate on my banister!"

Whoops. Johnny pulled back his smeary hand from the banister and ran upstairs.

Inside his bedroom, Ryan stared at the envelope.

Johnny trundled inside. His feet kicked aside the jeans Ryan had worn the day before, last Wednesday's T-shirt, and a pile of underwear that looked as if it had taken root in the carpet. Out of the tangle he pulled a small basketball and began shooting at a hoop on Ryan's wall.

"So, what's he have to say?" Johnny asked.

"Hold on." Ryan ripped open the envelope. A ticket folder fell out, emblazoned with the logo of an airline.

Johnny glanced over his shoulder. "Going somewhere?"

"Yeah," Ryan said, picking up the ticket. "China."

"Serious?"

"Over spring recess."

Johnny dropped the ball and plopped onto Ryan's bed. "Whoa! That's so cool! You and old pop saving the panda bear together."

Cool? Cool wasn't the word for it. No

word could describe how Ryan felt. Part of him wanted to dance on the roof. But another part of him was frustrated. Nothing else was in the envelope. No letter, no note.

Ryan sighed and glanced upward. On the ceiling, long ago, his father had hand-painted the constellations. *So you and I will always know we're looking at the same thing*, Dad had said.

Ryan knew every single star, every single mythical figure. He thought the memorizing would make him feel closer to his dad. But Dad had been gone so long, and it was hard to hold on to memories.

"It's no big deal," Ryan said with a shrug.

"How long has your dad been over there?" Johnny asked.

"Since he and Mom got divorced. About two years."

Beeeeep, went Ryan's watch.

BLLEEEEP! went Johnny's.

Uh-oh. Time to cut the small talk.

"*American Gladiators*," they said solemnly.

They charged down to the TV room.

Ryan made a mental note to set the

VCR. Spring break was three months away, but it was never too early to start preparing. Who knew if he'd have TV on the panda reserve? Going to China was fine — but *some* things, of course, could not be missed.

Chapter 2

Three months later.

Two eyes peer nervously out from the hollow of a tree. They take in the surrounding landscape — gnarled trees, thorny bushes, the bank of a river.

A flash of orange, by the water.

The panda fixes her gaze. She watches carefully as the orange glare fans into a plume of feathers. A pheasant waddles three or four steps to its left.

The panda relaxes. From between her legs, her chubby three-month-old male cub stumbles out of the hollow. He waddles toward the pheasant, attracted by the bright color.

Warning her son, the mother panda barks sharply. But the cub walks forward on young shaky legs.

With a loud flapping of wings against her barrellike body, the pheasant takes to the air.

The cub looks up to follow her flight. He falls on his behind.

Scrambling to his feet, the cub approaches the river. He looks into the gently rippling water and sees —

A small animal that looks like his mom! He reaches toward it — and it reaches toward him. He touches it. It ripples with the water. Delighted, he slaps it and almost falls in.

But his mom grabs him from behind. Playtime is over. Time for lunch.

The cub nurses as his mom collects bamboo. As she begins chewing on the stalks voraciously, she hears a rustling sound. A large animal.

In the distance she spots a pair of friendly musk deer. She relaxes.

But where is that smell coming from? Sniffing, the panda gazes around. Her eyes fix on a small hunk of dried meat. And another nearby. A whole trail of it.

It looks tasty. She shimmies between thick shrubs to move closer to it.

WHACK!

A heavy wooden gate smacks downward behind her. With a start, she looks frantically around. She is trapped in a log cage.

Panicked, she paws the slats in the cage, but they hold fast. She barks angrily, slamming her body against the wall. The cage shakes.

Outside, the little cub scurries up a tree. He watches with wide, confused eyes. He hears his mother's tortured cries, but somehow he knows he can do nothing to help.

Then, slowly, a small tube pokes through the slats of the cage. On the other side, a fifteen-year-old Chinese girl carefully puts her lips to the tube and aims it toward the raging panda.

The girl blows a short blast of air. A dart shoots out of the tube. It lodges in the fur around the mother panda's shoulder.

Her cries diminish, then stop. The panda struggles to remain upright, then slumps to the ground.

High above her, the little panda cub can no longer hear his mother. For the first time in his life, he feels sheer terror.

Chapter 3

Fifteen-year-old Ling Diao nervously twisted her blowpipe. Four men — including the American zoologist — were lifting the unconscious panda out of the cage and onto a large scale.

"Gently," grunted the American. "We don't want to hurt her."

Ling was only now becoming used to the rhythms of Dr. Michael Tyler's voice. He wasn't like anyone she'd ever met before, but she trusted him. She knew he was a friend of the pandas.

This panda was especially gorgeous. Ling stepped forward and patted it gently behind the ears. "She is so beautiful," she said.

The four scientists quickly went to work. Their time was limited before the panda would awaken from the sedative.

First they recorded her weight, then took her body measurements and her temperature. One of the men placed a white leather strap around her neck — a collar with a radio transmitter. He turned a plastic thumbscrew, and the collar's red indicator began to blink.

Another scientist gently pinched the panda's breast, extracting a drop of mother's milk.

"Either she's pregnant," Dr. Tyler said, "or she just had a cub."

Ling's face brightened. This was what everyone in the panda reserve had wanted. The Chinese government had funded the reserve under the condition that they begin breeding pandas. For so many years, that had been an almost impossible task. And now, a new cub! It was too good to be believed.

"A new cub would keep the reserve open," Ling remarked.

The panda slowly began to stir.

"She's fine," Dr. Tyler whispered. "Let's go."

Quickly Ling helped the men pack up the equipment. As they left for their tractor, no one saw the male panda cub, still in the tree.

If they had, they could not have helped but notice the look of relief on his tiny black-and-white face.

Chapter 4

"Good-bye, Gemini," said Ryan. Lying on his bed in the dark, he swung his flashlight to the right, until he found a telltale cluster of three stars on his ceiling. "Good-bye, Orion, good hunting." Another sweep of the light beam. "Good-bye, Big Dipper, don't spill anything while I'm gone. Good-bye, Ursa Minor, Little Bear."

Ryan shone the light on his night table clock. It read 2:30 A.M. In only a matter of hours, Ryan would be winging across the world.

Two years before, he had begged his dad to take him along to China. *A work trip* is what his dad had called it. He'd promised

to write. He'd promised to be home soon.
Well, "soon" had dragged into months and
years. Ryan wrote twice a week, hinting,
joking, *pleading* about a visit. Every day
he checked the mailbox for a response.

Over seven hundred days, exactly three
letters.

Three. Without one mention of a visit.

So Ryan had forgotten about it. And then
a ticket arrived. Great. As if Dad really
cared. Mom *must* have badgered him about
it. Ryan could just picture the visit —
hanging around smelly animal cages, catching an occasional glimpse of Dad at work,
if he was lucky.

Ryan sighed. Maybe it would be better
to stay home, where he was wanted.

The next morning, Ryan was up when
his mom peeked into his room. Sleep had
finally sneaked up on him last night. Un-
fortunately, it had brought him a nightmare. In it, Ryan had arrived at the airport
in China, and his dad was nowhere in sight.

Ryan's mind was made up. He would re-
fuse to go. But he'd have to break the news
gently to his mom, over breakfast.

In the kitchen, Mom was a bundle of

nerves. She would not eat. She raced around the house, finding medicines, throwing last-minute things into his bag, and barking out instructions and reminders. Ryan calmly waited for an opening, to break the news.

He was still waiting as they walked into the main concourse of the airport.

"Now, I sewed the name tags on all your underwear," she said for about the third time as they approached the ticket window. *Name tags, in China?* "Mom," Ryan said gently, "I was thinking — "

"Arrggghh, if they're not in Chinese, what good are they?" His mother closed her eyes, having realized her mistake. "Why didn't I think of that before?"

She fell silent as they joined the line at the ticket counter. *Now*, Ryan thought. *Tell her now.*

"Mom," he began, "I was thinking — "

"Remember, don't eat anything that has eyes," she interrupted. "And Daddy'll be right there at the gate the *second* you get off the plane. Oh, and if you get into trouble, call 911. I wonder if they have it over there. Just tell them you're an American."

"Mom, I don't really — "

"Next!" the ticket agent called to Mrs. Tyler.

She smiled and handed over Ryan's ticket.

"Window or aisle?" the agent asked.

"Aisle," Mrs. Tyler replied.

Ryan tugged at her coat. *"Mo-om!"*

"Smoking or non?" the agent asked.

Mrs. Tyler gave him a look. "He's twelve years old!"

"Mom, this is serious!" Ryan insisted.

"How many bags will you be checking in?" the agent barged on.

Mrs. Tyler reached for Ryan's duffel bag. Ryan stood in front of her and snatched the bag himself. "Mom, I don't want to go," he blurted.

"What?" His mom looked as if he'd just told her the sky was green.

"I don't want to go! I never did."

"Why did you wait till now to tell me?"

Ryan shrugged and looked downward.

"Come on, lady," urged the man behind them in line. "People who *do* want to go are getting impatient."

Mrs. Tyler grabbed Ryan's ticket away from the agent. "We'll be right back."

She took Ryan by the hand and led him

to a quiet spot by a plate glass window. "Sweetheart," she said softly, "I know it's frightening, going to a strange country on your own — "

"I'm not a little kid, Mom," Ryan replied. "I'm not scared."

"What is it, then? Don't you want to see your father?"

Ryan took a deep breath. "I don't think he wants to see me."

"Doesn't want to see you?" Mrs. Tyler repeated. "Of course he wants to see you. He sent you the tickets, didn't he?"

"Then how come, in two years, I wrote him forty-seven letters and he only answered three of them?"

Mrs. Tyler's expression softened. "Oh, honey. You know how you and Johnny get when you play Nintendo? You get so into it that hours go by and I have to come into the room and scream just to get you to notice me?"

Ryan nodded.

"Well, that's how your dad is with his work," Mrs. Tyler said.

"His work's more important to him than me?" Ryan shot back.

"No. But his work is so big that it blocks

out everything else. That doesn't mean he doesn't love you."

Yeah, right, Ryan wanted to say.

"This is going to date me," Mrs. Tyler went on, "but we used to have a saying: 'If you love something, set it free. If it comes back to you, then it's yours forever; if it doesn't, then it never was.' "

"It's been *two years*! How much longer do I have to wait for him to come back?"

Mrs. Tyler smiled compassionately. "You know how I know your father loves you? Because if he didn't, he wouldn't have risked breaking his neck to paint the constellations on your ceiling."

Ryan still wasn't convinced.

"Flight 23 to Hong Kong is now boarding through Gate 4C," a loudspeaker blared.

"That's your plane," Mrs. Tyler said. "Look, Ryan, planes work both ways. If you don't like it over there, you can always come home."

"Promise?" Ryan asked.

Mrs. Tyler nodded, her eyes moistening. She hugged her son and whispered, "I love you very much."

"I love you, too, Mom," Ryan replied.

When Mrs. Tyler pulled away, her

makeup was smeared with tears. She brushed them away, forced a smile, and said, "Be sure you brush your teeth *only* with bottled water."

A few minutes later, Ryan was fastened into a seat on Flight 23. He could see his mother's silhouette waving to him through an airport window. He waved back, trying to swallow the frog in his throat.

The plane taxied onto the runway, then took off. Ryan clutched his armrest. He'd never been on a plane before, never seen the ground so far below him. Now here he was, on the first leg of two flights: the first to Hong Kong, the second to Chengdu, where the Panda Reserve was located. He gulped hard, trying to keep his breakfast from making a reappearance.

A few minutes later a bland, cheerful voice came over the cabin speakers: "This is the captain. I've turned off the seat belt sign, so feel free to relax and get settled in."

Ryan tried to unstiffen his arms.

"We have seventeen hours to go," the captain added.

If I survive, Ryan said to himself.

Chapter 5

The mother panda pulls bamboo from the ground. Out of the corner of her eye, she watches her cub.

He is restless, scampering around the forest floor. Suddenly he stops. His body tenses, then he leaps.

A butterfly flutters away. The cub races after it, plunging into the surrounding brush.

The forest is full of dangers, and the mother panda does not want to lose sight of her cub. She barks a warning.

But the cub is having too much fun. He leaps and leaps after the butterfly, letting himself be drawn farther away.

The mother drops the bamboo and races after her child. Suddenly her body jerks. She falls to the ground.

Howling with pain, she looks at her left paw.

It is snared in a metal wire trap.

Chapter 6

"Thank you for flying with us," the flight attendant said as Ryan stepped out of the plane in Chengdu.

Ryan smiled wanly. His legs ached from the long trip, and he felt half asleep. As he emerged from the door, the sun glared in his eyes.

Where was the tunnel? Like the one he'd had to walk through to get to the plane in the United States?

In front of him, passengers were walking down a set of rickety metal stairs, right onto the runway. The airport building ahead looked more like a hut.

Slinging his duffel bag over his shoulder,

Ryan followed the others downward. As they filed across the runway, the ground began to rumble. An engine was roaring to their right.

Rolling toward him was a huge propeller plane. Ryan froze with panic. The man in front of him calmly stopped short.

VRRRRRRRRROOOOM!

In a flash, the plane passed in front of them and took flight. The crowd continued walking, as if nothing strange had happened.

"I have a feeling we're not in Kansas anymore, Toto." Wasn't that what Dorothy had said when she reached the Land of Oz? *That* was how Ryan felt.

Only worse. This was weirder than Oz.

Peering around the building, Ryan could see a throng of people in front — people with dead ducks slung over their shoulders, men pushing fruit carts, others riding horses or herding cattle. As Ryan approached the airport entrance, a guard with a rifle eyed him warily.

Inside the small building, people shoved and shouted. Ryan tried to read the signs, but not one of them was in English.

Go to the immigration desk with Dad as

soon as you get there, Ryan's mom had said. Well, Dad was nowhere to be seen, but Ryan spotted people of various nationalities lined up near an official-looking counter.

As Ryan joined the line, a hand landed on his shoulder.

Ryan spun around. The airport guard glowered at him, barking out something in Chinese.

"Uh, I have a passport," Ryan said, pulling his papers out of his jacket pocket.

The guard glanced at it. One by one, several other guards closed in. Ryan began sweating around the collar.

"Uh, I'm looking for my father," he tried. "Michael Tyler?"

The first official stared at him blankly.

"Michael Tyler?" Ryan repeated. "*Ty . . . ler*."

The official broke into a sudden smile. "Ahhhh," he said, nodding in recognition.

He pointed to his left. Smiling with relief, Ryan turned to see a door marked with a small silhouette.

"I said *Tyler*," Ryan grumbled. "Not *toilet*."

*　　*　　*

It took Ryan another hour to find the right lines to stand on and forms to fill out. Any second he expected his dad to step in and rescue him from the chaos.

But when Ryan finally left the airport, he was still alone.

He dodged bicycles and wooden carts. His eyes darted left and right.

Dad forgot. Ryan tried to force the thought out of his mind, but it hung there like a bad smell. *He was supposed to be here the second I got off the plane, but he forgot.*

Then, through the shifting horde, Ryan spotted a panda symbol on the side of a minibus!

"Dad!" Ryan shouted.

He ran to the bus and knocked on the side door.

It slid open. Inside, through a whirling cloud of cigarette smoke, several Chinese men in suits stared impatiently at him.

No Dad among them.

"Does this bus go to the panda reserve?" Ryan asked.

One of the men gestured to a seat.

Ryan sat in silence as the bus jounced over a rutted road, leading away from the airport.

At the panda reserve in Wolong, a scientist named Chang sat motionless, his eyes fixed on a large, electronic map. A few red lights blinked and moved slowly around.

Except for one. It had been in the same place for hours.

Behind him stood Ling Diao and another worker, Lei. They, too, looked at the red light with silent intensity.

As Dr. Michael Tyler approached, Ling blurted out, "Chang says the collar has not moved for a long time!"

"It is the mother panda we tagged three weeks ago," Lei reported.

Richard's face fell as he looked at the board. "And her cub is our only hope."

"Yes," Ling replied.

"We'll have to go out right away," Richard insisted, starting for the door.

Chang sprang into action, yelling out orders to the workers. A group of them obediently retrieved the panda-tracking equipment.

Ling ran outside. "Grandfather!" she called in Chinese.

On the dirt road in front of the reserve stood a broken-down tractor, hitched to a rickety trailer. From under the tractor, an old, wrinkled man slowly pushed himself into the light. "Eh?"

The workers were now rolling the equipment toward the tractor, led by Chang.

"A panda may be trapped in the forest," Ling explained urgently, in Chinese.

"We must hurry!" Chang added. "We've wasted too much time already!"

Ling's grandfather, Chu, was respected for his wisdom and quick thinking. He often went with the scientists into the forest. As the workers loaded the equipment onto the trailer, Chu helped tie it down.

When they were finished, Chu pulled a jar of murky, brownish liquid from an inner pocket. He took a quick swig, then licked his right index finger and held it in the air, concentrating intently.

After a moment he let the finger down and pronounced, in Chinese, "The time is right to go."

He hopped into the driver's seat of the tractor. Ling threw a backpack into the trailer, then climbed in beside Chu. Chang and Richard began hoisting themselves into the trailer.

But they all stopped at the sound of an approaching vehicle.

The government minibus pulled up to the reserve.

"Oh, no," Ling said to Richard. "The committee is early."

Ryan's face was pressed to the window of the minibus as it pulled up to the reserve. He spotted the old man in the tractor, but his attention was caught by the ponytailed American.

"Dad!" Ryan shouted.

Richard narrowed his eyes as he walked toward the bus. Ryan raced out the door to meet him, but his way was blocked by the officials stepping off.

"You're early," Richard remarked.

You're early? That wasn't the greeting Ryan had expected after two years, but hey, who cared? He was too psyched to be disappointed.

"A little," Ryan replied from behind one of the men. "The plane landed a few . . ."

His voice drifted off. His dad was looking at the officials, not him.

"Yes, Dr. Tyler," one of the men said. "We are here to make a preliminary report for Mr. Hsu on the progress of the reserve."

"But we aren't ready for an inspection," Richard insisted.

"We are only making a *preliminary* report," the man repeated. "Mr. Hsu will be here at the end of the week to make the final decision."

"No, that's not — " Richard stopped in midsentence. His eyes widened as he caught his first glimpse of his son. *"Ryan?"*

Ryan shouldered his way out from behind the officials. "It's me."

Richard threw his arms around Ryan. Ryan dropped his duffel bag and returned the hug, but quickly both of them pulled back. "What are you doing here?" Richard asked.

"You sent me a ticket," Ryan said with a shrug.

"But your plane's not due until eleven tonight."

"Eleven *this morning* you were supposed to meet me."

Richard blanched. "Jeez, Ryan, I'm sorry. How did you get here?"

"That bus."

"Oh, right. Good thinking."

"Dr. Tyler," one of the officials cut in, "I'm sorry to interrupt, but we cannot come back. We must inspect now."

"Look, gentlemen," Richard replied, "it was my understanding that this reserve was set up to save the panda. And right now I have a panda out there that might be in serious danger. So if you'll excuse me, I have to go. Chang can answer all your questions."

As the officials turned to Chang, Richard said, "Ryan, let's put your things in my room."

Ling picked up his duffel bag and tossed it to him. Ryan couldn't help but notice the cool, unfriendly look in her eyes.

What was going on here?

"Dad, I — " Ryan began.

But his father was already walking through the pagodalike entrance to the reserve compound.

Ryan ran to keep up. Richard led him past the panda enclosure, where workers wheeled barrows full of bamboo toward the cages.

"I'm sorry, Ryan," Richard said hurriedly, "it's just bad timing. I've got a situation here I've got to take care of. We'll be back before night, and then I promise we'll get caught up."

"Can't I go with you?" Ryan pleaded.

"No, it's too dangerous out there."

Richard led Ryan into a small, cramped hut. In the dim light, Ryan could make out a messed-up bed and a desk piled high with papers.

"You must be tired," Richard said. "Go take a nap or play with the bears. Watch out, some of them bite."

Ryan was speechless. He fought back the angry words that were bubbling up inside.

He noticed his dad's brow was all furrowed now — from what? Ryan wondered. Sympathy? Guilt? Maybe just indigestion.

"You'll be okay," Richard said gently. "I'll be back as soon as I can."

He attempted a smile, then walked out the door.

Ryan wandered glumly around the tiny room. No TV, no appliances, papers taped onto thin walls — the place looked so cheap and primitive.

He caught a glimpse of a familiar photograph in a frame on the desk. Picking it up, he looked at the two smiling faces in it — his and his dad's, years ago. Ryan remembered the shot. He'd been a kid. Innocent and contented. Not realizing that his best buddy was going to fly the coop.

Ryan threw the photo down.

"Seventeen hours on a plane," he blurted out to no one, "four hours on a bumpy bus, and bad airline food on top of it all. And for nothing!"

Cough-chukka-chukka-vrooom!

Outside, the tractor lurched to a start, belching blue-black smoke. Ryan watched it through the window. His dad was at the steering wheel, sitting next to Ling. Behind them sat Chu, on the trailer.

"Too dangerous, huh?" Ryan muttered. "It's not too dangerous for that girl and the old guy."

That did it. Ryan was not going to stay put another minute. He turned and bolted from the room.

Chapter 7

Outside, in the tractor, Richard clutched the steering wheel, praying the tractor would stay in one piece.

"Do you think the committee will give a good report?" Ling shouted over the engine noise.

"We didn't have a great year," Richard shouted back. "We weren't able to successfully impregnate Shen. We lost a ten-month-old cub for no apparent reason. And poachers took another two from the wild."

"Dad! Dad! Wait up!"

Richard looked over his shoulder to see

Ryan sprinting toward him. His jaw dropped.

In seconds Ryan was running alongside the slow tractor. "I didn't come all this way to stay in your crummy room and take a nap!" he shouted.

"Ryan, go back," Richard commanded. "It's just too dangerous in the forest."

Ryan pointed to Ling. "You're taking that funny-looking girl with you — *she's* no tougher than me. *I* can do it, too!"

Ling scowled at him, but Ryan didn't care. What was the difference? She probably couldn't understand English.

"Ryan, I don't have the time or patience for this right now!" Richard retorted. "Go back to the compound, and I *promise* I'll be back soon!"

Ryan stopped running. *"That's what you said two years ago!"*

Richard hit the brakes. The tractor swerved to a stop.

Ryan needed no further hint. His dad had that *hurry-up-before-I-change-my-mind* look.

As Ryan ran toward the tractor, Richard whispered something to Ling. Reluctantly she climbed out of the tractor and onto the trailer, next to Chu.

Ryan happily jumped into the seat next to his father.

Richard threw the tractor in gear.

Grinning, Ryan gazed at the lush scenery along the tight, dirt road. The forest seemed to close in, deep green and swaying with the wind. Around them, twigs snapped and leaves rustled, hinting at unseen animal life. Through breaks in the foliage, Ryan spotted mountainous peaks rising in the distance.

"How's your mother?" Richard asked.

"She's all right," Ryan replied. "I take care of her."

Behind them, Ryan could hear Ling complaining to Chu. He glanced back a moment and saw her bouncing uncomfortably up and down, clutching the sides of the trailer.

Ryan gave her a friendly smile. She sneered back.

"Is she mad or something?" Ryan asked.

"Probably," his dad replied.

"What does she do?"

"Ling works as my translator. Chu is her

grandfather. He's been working with the pandas all his life."

Ryan's face turned red. "Translator? She speaks English?"

Richard nodded.

Ryan sneaked a glance backward again. Ling wasn't *that* funny-looking.

Ugh. What a way to make friends. *She hates my guts now*, Ryan thought.

He fell silent as the tractor began climbing a steep hill. Richard shifted into low gear. The engine groaned and wheezed. The trailer hitch squeaked.

Soon the tractor almost came to a stop. Ryan was afraid it wouldn't make it. He held tightly to the fender, tensing his body in case he had to jump.

SNNNNNAP!

The tractor jolted forward.

"YEEEAAAAHHH!"

Ryan spun around at the sound of Chu and Ling's screams.

The hitch had snapped. The trailer was rolling back downhill, picking up speed as it bounced over ruts. Ling and Chu were holding on for dear life, their faces taut with fear.

Richard stopped the tractor. He and Ryan jumped out and chased after the run-away trailer.

Ryan's feet pounded the old road. He watched in horror as the trailer headed for a sharp bend.

Thump! It struck the road's embankment and lurched into the air.

Ling and Chu flew off. They tumbled onto the road as the trailer bounced onto a nearby field and overturned.

As Ryan and his dad drew nearer, Chu struggled to his feet. His face twisted with fury, he ranted in Chinese, shaking his fist.

"Are you all right?" Richard asked Ling, panting for breath.

Ling nodded.

Richard looked relieved. He gave Chu a swift glance, ignoring the torrent of words, then turned back to the tractor. "I'll back it up," he said.

Ryan helped Chu and Ling retrieve the trailer. Together they hooked it back onto the tractor. Chu complained bitterly the whole time, never stopping, never running out of breath.

After a while, Ryan tuned him out. The old man was a talker. Big-time.

Ryan wished he'd remembered to bring earplugs.

A short distance away, the mother panda nurses her cub. The little one's eyes dart anxiously toward the wire snare that has bloodied his mother's wrist. She rocks him, desperately trying to provide comfort.

She needs comfort herself, though. And not only because of the painful trap.

Something is moving among the trees. The cub does not yet notice, but the mother is riveted. She watches a dark, long form move through the leaves. It is edging nearer, staying out of sight.

For hours the mother panda watches. The stalker is in no hurry to leave. But it is not yet attacking. Perhaps it does not see the snare; it does not understand that the panda is trapped. It is waiting for the panda to drop her guard, turn her back, perhaps fall asleep.

The panda struggles against fatigue. Her cub is heavy, and her injured arm flares with pain.

It is becoming harder and harder to stay awake. The panda's eyelids flutter, then close. Her head sinks, but only for a moment.

In that moment, a leopard leaps out of the brush, its claws slicing the air!

Chapter 8

CRRRACK!

When the rifle shot resounded, Ryan, his father, Chu, and Ling were loading the tracking equipment onto the trailer.

They stopped and looked up. In the distance, a cloud of frightened birds swept upward from a treetop.

"What was that?" Ryan asked.

Chu muttered an answer in Chinese.

Ryan frowned. "Huh?"

"Give me the blowgun!" ordered his dad.

Impatiently he reached into the trailer and pulled out the small pipe himself.

"But it might be dangerous," Ling warned.

Ryan was scared and confused. "Dad, what's she talking about?"

"Poachers," his father replied.

Chu spoke up agitatedly.

"He says it's too dangerous to go," Ling translated.

"I'll be all right," Richard insisted. "You guys stay here."

Richard walked into the thick undergrowth, leaving Ryan alone with Chu and Ling. Neither of them seemed too pleased with the idea.

For the first time, he wished he were back in his father's cramped room at the reserve.

Deeper in the forest, the mother panda sat staring. The leopard was a lifeless heap at the edge of the clearing, a bullet hole in its chest.

Her cub sat next to her, not quite daring to move.

Slowly, through the surrounding growth, a pair of humans walked closer. One of them held a smoking rifle.

The mother panda struggled against her manacle. She angled her body protectively in front of her cub.

Shong and Po had been hunting rare animals for months. In their hideout, they had a collection of furs and horns. All were taken from protected species. Protected ones were the best, as far as Shong and Po were concerned. Killing them was illegal — which translated into big money on the black market.

As long as you weren't caught.

Shong lowered his rifle and smiled. This was too good to be true. The mother panda was weak. Killing her would be easy, and her pelt would fetch a high price. But a live panda cub — *that* would make them rich.

Po approached the panda. With her tired, weakened muscles, she drew her cub closer.

Po gripped the little cub, who wriggled in terror. With a grunt, he yanked the cub away. Ignoring its squeals, he stuffed the male cub in a knapsack and returned to Shong.

Now for the mother. Shong raised his rifle, aiming at the panda's head.

As the panda tried to turn away, Po suddenly pointed out the panda's collar.

It beeped a steady, red, electronic signal.

Po knew the penalty for killing a panda in China. If this panda were traced to them, they would be sentenced to death.

"Let's go," Po said in Chinese. "The cub is enough."

But Shong pushed him away and tightened his trigger finger.

Richard crept through the forest, holding the tracking antenna over his head. His readings were clear. The panda couldn't be more than a few yards away.

He pushed aside a thick bush and gasped.

In the clearing, two poachers stood over a trapped panda, one of them aiming a rifle.

"No!" Richard blurted without thinking. "Don't shoot!"

He dropped the antenna and ran into the clearing.

Startled, Shong swung his rifle toward Richard.

Too late. Richard leaped on him, forcing him to the ground.

Shong held tight to the rifle. In desperation, he squeezed the trigger.

CRRRACK!

"Aaaggh!" Dr. Tyler clutched his leg and fell away. Shong sprang to his feet.

"Let's get out of here!" Po shouted frantically in Chinese. "Leave him to die!"

As Richard writhed on the ground, the two poachers sprinted into the forest.

Chapter 9

At the sound of the shot, Ryan tensed.

"Dr. Tyler!" Ling screamed.

She was the first to run into the woods. Chu followed.

For a moment Ryan could not move. He felt dizzy. This was not real. It couldn't be.

He unlocked his knees and sped after the other two.

Ling and Chu arrived at the clearing first. Richard was groaning with pain, a few feet away from the panda. Blood seeped through his hands where they clutched his pant leg.

Ling raced to his side. "Dr. Tyler, are you all right?"

"Yes," Richard replied through gritted teeth. "There were two of them. They have her cub."

Ryan stopped at the edge of the clearing. His father was alive! Relief washed over him. He wanted to run to his dad and hug him, but he didn't. Something inside stopped him. It would be too embarrassing. He would get in the way. Better to let Chu and Ling help him.

They knew him better.

Chu said something sharply to his granddaughter in Chinese. Immediately she removed her bandanna and gave it to him.

With swift, strong motions, Chu wrapped the bandanna around Richard's leg to stop the bleeding.

"They . . . took the cub," Richard grunted, pointing into the forest.

"I'm worried about *you*," Ling replied.

"Don't," Richard said. "The bullet only grazed my leg."

Again Chu spoke to his daughter in Chinese.

Ling nodded. "I will radio for a helicopter," she explained.

As she ran off, Chu pulled a jackknife

from an inner pocket. He began hacking away at the panda's trap.

Richard's eyes were fixed on the panda. "We have to save her for the cub's sake!" he said urgently.

He's been shot. He's bleeding. And all he can think about is a stupid panda bear.

More than ever, Ryan realized how little he understood his dad.

Before long the shuddering noise of a helicopter broke the forest's silence. By that time, Chu had freed the panda, and she lay close to Richard.

As the chopper descended into the clearing, the treetops bent away in the powerful draft.

The moment it touched ground, Lei jumped out of the pilot's seat. He and Chu struggled to lift the heavy panda into the helicopter's cabin.

"Take her collar off!" Richard urged. "It'll help her breathe a little easier!"

Ling rushed over, unclasped the collar, and pulled it off. She pressed the OFF button and the blinking light stopped. Then she opened her backpack and stuffed the collar in.

Lei and Chu now helped Richard hobble toward the helicopter.

Gritting his teeth in agony, Richard asked, "Where's Ryan?"

Ryan stepped out from his place near the bushes, into the light.

"There you are," Richard said. "You get in front."

Ryan walked toward the chopper, but Lei held out his arm to stop him. "No. There's too much weight already."

"What's wrong?" Richard asked.

"Too much weight for the helicopter!" Lei repeated, shouting to be heard above the noise of the blades. "No room for the boy!"

Richard gripped the doorjamb. "Take Ryan back, and I'll wait here."

"I will drop you and the bear off," Lei insisted. "Then I will come back."

"No!" Richard protested. "Ryan can't stay here."

Ryan finally spoke up. "I can wait here, Dad."

Lei was climbing into the pilot's seat. "We must hurry!"

"Okay," Richard said to Ryan, "but stay right here. *Don't move from this spot.*"

"Don't worry about that," Ryan said.

"Lei will be right back to pick you up."

Lei pulled the chopper door shut, cutting off the conversation.

Ryan watched as the helicopter rose upward. He kept his eyes on it until it disappeared into the sinking afternoon sun.

Chapter 10

Ryan hadn't felt so weird since the last junior high dance. Ling was staring off into the woods, as if she hadn't yet noticed he was there. He wanted to talk to her but felt tongue-tied.

This is ridiculous, Ryan said to himself. *You are the only two people here!*

Well, sort of. Chu was there, too, but at the moment he seemed to be doing some ancient imitation of a garden slug. He was on all fours, crawling slowly around the clearing, his face only inches off the ground.

"Lose a contact?" Ryan asked.

Chu scowled at him briefly.

Ryan watched for a few moments, then finally asked Ling, "What's he doing?"

Chu leaped to his feet. Ryan stepped back, thinking he was about to be attacked.

Instead, Chu and Ling began speaking in rapid, excited Chinese.

"*What?*" Ryan asked.

Suddenly Chu scurried into the forest.

"Hey!" Ryan shouted. "Where's he going?"

Ling sighed. "My grandfather says he found the poachers' trail. They're headed for the ravine. They couldn't have gotten very far."

"But — the rifle — " Ryan stammered.

"He says the cub will die without mother's milk." Ling shrugged. "He's right. We must bring the cub back to the reserve."

"But you can't leave me!" Ryan insisted.

"Then come," Ling said.

"Are you crazy? I'm not risking my life for some old panda bear!"

"Fine. Stay here. Make yourself happy."

Ling picked up the blowpipe, which had fallen into the sparse grass. Lifting her chin defiantly, she took off after Chu.

"Fine. Go." Ryan folded his arms. "Who needs you? I'll have you know, I earned a couple of merit badges from the Boy Scouts! *I can handle the wild!*"

Ryan was rooted. No way was he going into a dark forest, chasing after armed killers. No way in the world was he going to defy his dad. He was going to stay put and greet that helicopter when it came back. It would serve Ling right if she got lost.

Or worse.

The sound of Ling's footsteps quickly died out. A bird cawed. A bug the size of a small rodent buzzed Ryan's face. He swatted it away.

Behind him the leaves began to rustle.

Ryan whirled around. Was that a movement? What was that shadow?

"Ling?" Ryan's voice was a frightened squeak. "Oh, Ling?"

"YEEEAAAAK!"

An animal leaped out of the brush.

Ryan screamed and jumped away.

He caught a glimpse of a golden monkey, swinging from tree to tree. It chattered merrily, as if it were laughing at him.

Ryan swallowed hard. "He said to stay here," he muttered to himself. "It's perfectly safe."

Right.

Shadows seemed to lurk behind every tree. Bizarre noises closed in around him.

"Hello, 911?" Ryan said under his breath. "I don't know where I am. Somewhere in the mountains where nobody speaks English. And there're bears out here. And men with guns — "

Ryan felt something slither over his sneakers. He looked down at a large, slimy snake.

He gasped, too terrified to move.

". . . And a snake's crawling across my feet."

That did it.

"Wait up for me!" he bellowed, bolting into the woods.

Ling and Chu had trampled down some grasses here and there. Ryan tried to follow their path, using his Boy Scout skills.

But they only helped him for a few yards. Before long, every inch of the ground looked fresh and untrod.

"Ling? Chu?" he called. "Where'd you guys go?"

Whomp! Ryan's foot caught on a tree root and he thudded to the forest floor.

As he rose to his feet, he heard another rustling noise. Near him.

He looked into a bamboo patch and saw a tiny shoot wriggling wildly, as if it were dancing.

"What the — ?" Ryan began.

Fiiiish!

The shoot disappeared downward, into the ground.

Ryan jumped back.

What kind of place was this? Even the plants were alive!

His hope was draining fast. Tears began to cloud his vision. He opened his mouth to make a desperate cry for help.

But he cut himself off.

He was picking up voices. Distant, but close enough to know they weren't speaking English.

Ryan stood up and quietly plodded through a thicket of trees. The voices became louder, mixing now with the rushing noise of water.

Before long, light streamed through the tangle of branches before him. He walked into a grassy area that dropped off steeply to a raging river.

But Ryan was not noticing the river at all. His eyes were focused on a bridge that crossed over the canyon. It was made of metal wire, drooping dangerously and barely supporting a walkway of wooden planks.

Walking across it, holding a heavy sack, were the two poachers. Ryan could see the panicky movements of the small cub inside the sack.

No time to think. Ryan raised his fingers to his mouth and blew.

The whistle echoed through the canyon.

"Hey!" Ryan shouted. "Over — "

From behind him, a hand reached around and clamped over his mouth.

Ryan was pulled back farther into the woods. He jerked his head around. He came face to face with Chu.

His wrinkled face contorted with anger, Chu scolded him, muting his words through a screen of bared, rotten teeth.

Ryan didn't mind the hand. Or the furious words. It was the breath that nearly knocked him out.

What was *in* that bottle of brown liquid this guy drank?

When Chu finally let go, Ryan pulled away. He spotted Ling near a bush. She was grim-faced and tense, peering out toward the bridge.

"What'd your grandfather say?" Ryan asked.

" 'Shut up,' " Ling translated.

"Oh."

Ryan watched the two men on the bridge. They were looking around suspiciously. Then, seeing nothing, they grunted at each other, continued across, and disappeared into the forest on the other side.

"These are poachers," Ling said.

Duh, Ryan thought.

Chu licked his finger and held it up again, concentrating intently. Then he pulled out his bottle and took a swig of the muddy liquid.

Ryan felt sick.

As Chu stepped toward the grassy area near the bridge, he gestured for Ryan and Ling to follow.

Ling obeyed immediately.

No way was Ryan going to be left behind again. He walked close behind Ling, stepping over tangled vines and twisted branches.

When they reached the grassy area, he had a clearer look at the bridge. The wire was rusty and corroded. Many of the wooden planks had fallen; those still left were ancient and rotting. The thieves had taken a big risk crossing over.

Chu stepped briskly onto the bridge, not even looking down.

"Go," Ling urged.

What?

Ryan's stomach almost pole-vaulted into his throat. This was crazy.

Still, the old man was having no trouble walking, and if he could do it . . .

Holding on to the wire support, Ryan took a tentative step.

Screeeeeak!

The bridge creaked, swaying to the right.

Ryan's knuckles whitened as he tightened his grip on the wire.

He took another step, and another. The bridge swung. The wooden planks spat splinters into the river as they slipped beneath him.

"Uh, maybe we should wait for the helicopter to come back," Ryan said, turning to Ling.

"By then, it will be too late," Ling replied. "Are you going or not?"

"Look at this thing! It's ancient."

"It's safe! See Grandfather?"

Ryan gazed back to the other side. Chu was on the bank, waving agitatedly.

"Go on," Ling insisted.

Ryan took a few measured breaths. *Steady*, he told himself. *Place your feet and go.*

He looked down to find a secure plank.

Big mistake.

Through the gaps, Ryan could see the raging current below. *Far* below.

The breath caught in his throat. His knees locked.

"Don't look down," came Ling's voice from behind him.

"It's a little too late for that!" Ryan retorted.

Now Chu was shouting at them.

"I can't hear what he says," Ling complained. She scrinched up her face, straining to hear. Then her eyes widened. "Hurry! I think he says the panda cub is in trouble!"

The stupid panda again. Ryan shook his head. "Sorry, but there's no way I'm crossing this bridge."

He turned back to step off.

But something was waiting for him. It

had the face of a goat, the body of a bull, sharp horns — and eyes that said, *You're history*, *pal*.

"Yeeeeaaaaagh!" Ryan screamed.

"Run!" Ling yelled.

She took off toward her grandfather.

Ryan's ankles were locked. It was either run over the bridge of doom or be barbecued.

The hulking takin lowered its horns and pawed the ground.

"He's going to charge!" Ling shrieked.

With a sudden thrust of its hind legs, the animal leaped onto the bridge.

Chapter 11

Ryan turned and ran.

Planks splintered and dropped into the river. Behind Ryan and Ling, the takin galloped. Ryan lurched about with the sudden, heavy movement.

Panting, he and Ling reached the other side. Chu's eyes were still on the bridge. Ryan glanced over his shoulder. The takin had stopped. It was now staring downward, through a gap in the planks that Ryan and Ling had made.

The creature stayed there for a moment. Then it turned and sulked back to the other side.

Chu burst into laughter.

"That thing almost killed us," Ryan said through gasping breaths. "What's so funny?"

Chu spoke to Ling, and she explained, "Grandfather thought it was funny."

Ryan frowned. "Glad *he's* having fun."

Chuckling, Chu led them into the woods. He scampered lightly over the rough terrain, twisting and turning as if following a scent. Ling tripped twice but kept up. Ryan's feet sank into ruts. Thorns scratched him all over. Low branches conked him on the head. He was convinced his ankles would never be the same.

It seemed like hours before Chu stopped.

In front of them, partially hidden by branches, was a small, dark opening in a boulder. Chu once again licked his finger and held it high.

"Is there, like, radar in his finger?" Ryan asked.

Ling only replied, "Grandfather is very wise."

Chu exclaimed and pointed upward, to a spot beyond the boulder. Thin, gray tendrils of smoke wound slowly upward.

All three of them walked closer, crouching low. Chu whispered to Ling.

"What'd he say?" Ryan asked.

"This is the poachers' cave," Ling answered.

Smoke. That meant a fire. That meant someone was inside. Someone not likely to be welcoming visitors at that moment. "So," Ryan said, "now that we know where they live, why can't we go back, report them to the panda police, and let them take it from here?"

"It's not so easy," Ling replied.

Chu motioned for them to follow. He led them to a secluded area behind a thicket. Ryan and Ling crouched there, staring at the cave through the leaves.

Chu walked to a large tree. He stood inches away, gazing into the gnarled bark.

"What's he doing?" Ryan asked.

"He is thinking up a plan to rescue the cub," Ling said.

Ryan nodded. "Or maybe he's just staring at a tree and doesn't have any clue about what to do."

Chuck-a-chuck-a-chuck-a-chuck . . .

Ryan looked up. Above them, the distant sound of a helicopter was drawing nearer.

In moments, the panda reserve chopper raced into view over the tall trees.

"It's the helicopter!" Ryan cried, running out of the thicket.

"No!" Ling shouted.

Ryan didn't care who saw him. That chopper was their only chance. He ran into a clearing, waving his arms wildly.

"Hey!" he shouted at the top of his lungs. "Down here!"

Chu and Ling raced over to him, urging him in two languages to be quiet.

"We have to make sure he sees us!" Ryan said.

"No, stop!" Ling insisted. "The *poachers* will see us!"

Chu was yelling at his granddaughter in Chinese, gesticulating wildly.

Ryan ignored them. "I've got to get out of here!" he proclaimed, jumping up and down, flailing with his arms.

Ling leveled her eyes at him, coolly.

Then, without a trace of emotion, she reared back and socked him in the face.

Ryan fell to the ground.

In the panda reserve hospital, Richard watched closely as Chang stitched the mother panda's wounds.

Leaning on a cane, Richard took weight

off his injured leg. The operating table was nothing more than a wooden plank, but Richard had faith in Chang's skills. The sutures looked clean and even.

Chih was going to be all right.

On the helicopter ride home, Chang had thought up the panda's name. Chih had been a family name; it had belonged to Chang's grandmother, the toughest and wisest person he had ever known.

"Hang in there, Chih," Richard said. "You're doing great."

He wasn't sure the panda had heard him. She was heavily anesthetized. Her eyes were glazed and half-open.

The sound of an approaching helicopter drew away Richard's attention.

He hobbled toward the door. They had taken a long time. Surely Ryan hadn't wandered from the clearing. He was a smart boy. He'd never pull something strange in a situation like that.

Would he?

At the door, Richard watched the chopper touch down. As the rotors slowed, Lei stepped out.

No one else followed.

Using his cane for balance, Richard hurried to Lei. "Where are they?" he called.

"I am so sorry," Lei replied, his brow furrowed. "I could not find them and the boy."

Richard felt his insides clutch. "What do you mean, you can't find them?"

"I went to the spot. I circled many times. I did not see them."

"They *had* to be there."

"No. Maybe they built camp for the night. They got tired and will sleep in the forest tonight."

"We need to go back!" Richard pleaded.

"No." Lei pointed toward the darkening sky. "It's night. We can't see. We will go back in the morning."

"I *told* him to wait there."

"Do not worry," Lei reassured him. "The boy is safe with Chu and Ling."

Richard nodded. Lei was right. Flying at night would be useless. The forest would be one big shadow. Besides, Chu and Ling knew the forest, and they were good guides.

On the other hand, Ryan had hardly been out of the suburbs his whole life.

Richard limped back into the building. He knew he wouldn't have a moment of sleep that night.

Chapter 12

Ryan's eyes fluttered open. As they focused into wakefulness, he could hear the chirping and cawing of the forest birds.

Around him were dim gray rock walls. He sat up with a start. Was he in the poachers' cave? Had he been captured?

Where were Chu and Ling?

Ling. The thought of her made his jaw ache. He rubbed it, feeling the sharp pain of a bruise.

Struggling to his feet, Ryan walked to the opening of the stone dwelling. He felt groggy and stiff, as if he'd spent the night sleeping on solid rock.

Which, considering the bright daylight outside, was probably exactly what had happened.

Stepping into the forest morning was like taking a warm shower. The air was cool, the sunlight warming. Mountain streams burbled nearby, and the dew tickled his feet.

On a patch of dirt beside the cave, Chu practiced a *tai chi* routine. He was alone, and he looked unafraid.

Ryan exhaled with relief. The poachers were nowhere to be seen. Now he realized, too, that the cave was not the same one they had seen the evening before; Chu and Ling had found another one and somehow dragged Ryan along with them.

Maybe the old man had fed the crooks some of his brown liquid and sent them off screaming for mercy.

When Ryan smiled, his jaw twinged with pain. The girl had really socked him.

He could not take his eyes off Chu. The old man's movements were fluid, like a dancer's — except he was moving so slowly.

"They call *that* exercise?" Ryan muttered to himself. What a piece of cake.

He studied Chu a moment, just in case there was any sudden complicated twist to the exercise.

Nahhh.

Ryan walked up to Chu. The old man didn't seem to see him at all.

Chu lifted his right leg, drawing back his left hand.

Ryan did the same, wobbling on his ankle. He copied Chu as he brought his arms and legs around, slooooowly turning . . .

Right into the gaze of Ling.

She was standing against a boulder, arms folded, smiling. A big, mocking, *what-a-dork* kind of smile.

Yikes.

Ryan pushed right through the *tai chi* movement, as if he were just on the way to a big, wide, morning stretch.

"Aaaaaaaaah!" *Great yawn*, Ryan complimented himself. *Academy Award time.* "What's up?"

Ling didn't look too convinced. She walked toward him, suddenly pulling her hand from behind her back.

Ryan flinched. "You're not going to hit me again, are you?"

"It depends if you do something stupid or not," Ling answered.

Whoa, did this little kid think *she* was cool. "Yeah, well, you sucker-punched me anyway," Ryan said. "I never had a chance."

Ling was holding out a withered brown strip of dried meat in her outstretched hand. "This is breakfast," she said.

"No, this is *beef jerky*," Ryan corrected her. "*Breakfast* is blueberry pancakes with maple syrup, bacon on the side, and two eggs over easy." He grabbed the beef jerky out of her hand and held it up. "This is a treat you give your dog when he rolls over."

"So roll over," Ling replied, "then eat it."

"It tastes like my baseball mitt!"

Before Ling could answer, Chu walked up to her with a question. They talked in Chinese for a moment, and Chu laughed as he gestured to Ryan.

"What's he saying about me?" Ryan asked.

"I told grandfather I spied on the poachers and saw them leaving the cave to go hunting," Ling said. "He says since you practiced *tai-chi*, you are now a warrior ready to battle the poachers."

Ryan took a deep gulp. Warrior? Him? Uh-uh.

If the old man thought that goony *tai chi* stuff was going to make *Chu* strong, then they were all looking for trouble. Big trouble.

Ling and Chu padded quietly through the brush. Ryan followed close behind, keeping low when he caught sight of the poachers' cave.

Outside the entrance, Shong sat against the rock face, snoozing.

"I thought you said they were gone!" Ryan whispered.

"They must have come back," Ling replied.

Chu said something to her in Chinese and walked off.

"He's leaving us?" Ryan asked in a panic.

"He will watch out for the other poacher," Ling explained. "If he sees him, he will whistle to warn us." She motioned Ryan toward her. "Come. We must get closer."

Ling turned away from Ryan and tiptoed up a small incline, toward the cave.

Ryan fought the urge to run. He couldn't let Ling do this alone. He forced himself to follow her up the incline.

Keeping her eyes on the sleeping crook, Ling crept closer, her feet touching lightly into whatever footholds they found — a root, a rock . . .

Ling pushed too hard against a large loose rock. To Ryan's horror, it broke loose from the soil and tumbled noisily downhill.

Shong's eyes opened. He sat up with a start and looked around.

Ling and Ryan silently hit the deck.

"Po?" Shong called out.

No reply.

Between two roots, Ryan could see Shong standing up. He took another look into the woods, then walked into the cave.

"What if he's going to get his partner?" Ryan asked.

Ling shushed him.

A moment later Shong emerged. In his right hand was a rifle.

Ryan felt sick. His body shook.

Shong stalked along the side of the cave. He passed a few feet in front of Ryan and Ling. His eyes scanned the forest as he slowly brought the rifle around, left to right.

Then he stopped abruptly. Ryan closed his eyes.

When he opened them, Shong had turned back toward the cave wall. He sat back down and yawned. Placing the rifle close beside him, he fell asleep.

Gradually Ryan's blood started flowing again.

"How do you expect us to take him?" he whispered.

Wordlessly, Ling reached into her backpack and pulled out the blowpipe. Smiling, she showed it to Ryan.

Nuts, Ryan thought. *She is totally out of her mind.*

This dude did *not* look like the type you fought with a toy.

Silently they approached Shong along the edge of the woods. His snores became louder.

When they were as close as they dared go, Ling raised the pipe to her lips. Shong was at a funny angle, his face turned away and partially blocked by a bump in the rock.

"What is that thing, anyway?" Ryan asked.

Ling ignored him. She aimed carefully, stretching her body to get the best trajectory.

"Maybe we should just go," Ryan suggested.

"Ssssh!" Ling admonished him out of the side of her mouth.

"He has a gun, with real bullets! And what are you going to do with that thing? Hit him with a spitball?"

Ling removed the pipe and looked at Ryan with sharp disappointment. "You are nothing like your father. Dr. Tyler is brave."

The words hit Ryan like a sledgehammer.

Not brave? Who did she think she was? Maybe he hadn't *seemed* brave so far. But hey, this was a strange place. Far away, full of dangers. If Ling were in the United States, she'd be scared of stuff, too — he couldn't think of *what*, exactly, but there had to be something.

"The angle is no good," Ling muttered, straining to line up the blowpipe with Shong. "He needs to be more to the left."

Ryan eyed the sleeping gunman. Moving closer would be risky. The guy would see them, for sure. Ling certainly wasn't going to try that.

But someone *braver* would.

Ryan stood up. It was time for action. No more Mr. Nice Chicken. If it was bravery Ling wanted to see, bravery she'd get.

"Hey, you stupid poacher!" Ryan taunted, leaping out of their hiding place.

Shong's eyes flickered open.

Ryan raced toward the cave. "Over here, dorkbrain!"

Ling looked on in utter disbelief. "Oh, no," she murmured.

Shong was on his feet now, gun in hand.

"Yo, genius," Ryan shouted, near the cave entrance. "I'm here!"

"That boy is crazy," Ling whispered to herself.

She watched as Shong passed in front of her. He stopped at a corner of the rock wall. As he leaned cautiously around it, he disappeared more or less from the waist up.

But not from the waist down.

Ling had her target. A big one.

She inhaled and lifted her pipe.

At that moment, Ryan ran out from behind the rock — right into Shong's sight. Shong aimed his rifle.

"Yeeeeeaggggh!" Ryan screamed, running frantically into the woods.

Ling blew. The dart went flying.

Thoop! It lodged just below Shong's belt.

Ling held her breath. Shong was turning, keeping Ryan in his rifle sight. Suddenly he paused. One hand reached around, feeling the back of his pants. His fingers closed around the dart.

His hand stayed there a moment. Then, with a thump, Shong collapsed to the ground.

Stumbling through the woods, Ryan looked over his shoulder. Ling was standing over Shong's slumped body. She kicked the rifle away from him, then picked it up.

Ryan stopped running. His heart felt like a V-8 engine as he walked toward the cave.

For the first time since they'd met, Ling smiled at him. Ryan shrugged and raised his eyebrows nonchalantly.

Piece of cake.

Silently Ling gestured for him to follow. Ryan stayed close behind her as they walked into the mouth of the cave.

The hideout was cold and empty, receding into darkness. Ryan snooped around, peering at the shadows.

The place gave Ryan the creeps. "Looks like we got the wrong cave," he said, "because I don't see any cub here."

But now Ryan's eyes were adjusting to the dark. A dim light shone from the back of the cave. Together he and Ling walked toward it.

As they stepped into a small area near an almost burned-out fireplace, Ryan's breath hitched in his throat.

Lying all over the floor were animal hides — leopard, monkey, bear, and many Ryan couldn't even recognize. All were strewn about in messy, bulky piles.

Ling set the rifle down by a rock. She walked to one of the piles and lifted up two hides.

They were black and white and gorgeous.

Ryan ran his fingers through the lustrous fur of the slaughtered panda. He felt a sickening pang in his gut.

"Why do they want these?" Ryan asked.

"To sell." Ling's eyes filled with tears. She let go of the hides and turned away.

"Do you think one of these is the cub?"

"No. They want the cub to sell to a zoo."

Ling's face went slack. Her eyes fixed on a basket in a corner of the cave.

A basket that seemed to be moving.

Ling ran to it and began struggling with the ropes that held it shut.

"I can get it," Ryan volunteered.

Ling stepped aside. Ryan tugged and pulled to no avail.

"You're making it worse," Ling complained.

"Go check Sleeping Beauty," Ryan said. "See if he's got a knife on him."

Ling ran to the cave opening. Shong was snoring. She yanked the dart out of his rear, then searched his back pockets.

"Hurry up," Ryan urged from inside. "I don't want to be here when his friend comes back."

Rolling Shong over, Ling reached into his front pockets. Nothing.

What kind of poacher didn't carry a knife? Surely there must be some sort of sharp tool around.

But as she stood up, a shadow loomed on the cave wall. A shadow of a man with a rifle.

Chapter 13

"Aaagh!" Ling gasped, whirling around.

Chu stared back at her. He smiled, bemused.

"Don't *ever* do that!" Ling ranted to him in Chinese. "You nearly scared me to death!"

Inside the cave, Ryan's forehead dripped with sweat. His fingers had found the loosest part of the rope. It was slowly coming undone.

With a final grunt, he pulled it off.

The top popped open. With a violent lurch, the basket rolled away.

Ryan fell back onto the dirt floor. His baseball cap went flying.

When he looked up, he saw a small, shivering shape near the basket. Its black-and-white fur shone dully in the room's dim light, but in its eyes was an unmistakable, burning fear.

Ryan couldn't help but stare. The mother panda had been stunning and majestic. But this cub, so fragile and doll-like, took Ryan's breath away.

"So that's what all the fuss is about," Ryan said in awe.

Ling and Chu ran up beside him. Despite their years of travel in the Szechwan forest, despite all their work in the panda reserve, they, too, could only stare in silent wonderment.

Chu lifted the cub, examined it briefly, then spoke to Ling.

"Grandfather says the cub needs milk," she said. "We must get it back to its mother quickly."

"What about these hides?" Ryan asked. "We'll need them to nail these guys."

"No, it's too much to carry," Ling replied. "We can only take the cub."

Chu scooped up the cub in his arms and rushed out of the cave entrance. Ling and Ryan were right on his heels. The cub whimpered and looked around in confusion.

On her way out, Ling paused by the inert, sleeping poacher. Looking at him, thinking about what he'd had in mind for the cub, her face reddened with anger.

Before she moved on, she gave him a swift kick in the gut.

Chu led them into the forest. At the bottom of a long incline, they veered off into a dense area of trees.

Ryan kept his eyes on the ground. With every few steps, the forest seemed to become darker and more overgrown. Even though it was midmorning, it felt like nighttime.

After what seemed like hours, Chu stopped walking. He set the cub down on the ground and mumbled something to his granddaughter.

"Grandfather must rest awhile," Ling said, helping the old man sit down.

Ryan perched on a rock. He was tired, sweaty, and thirsty.

Catching his breath, he watched the male cub walk around — first on shaky legs, and then more freely.

The panda cub wandered over to a small patch of bamboo, then stopped. His body tensed slightly.

Ryan looked at the bamboo. One of the shoots was wiggling, just like the one he'd seen earlier!

As Ryan leaned closer, the shoot vanished into the ground. The cub jumped back in surprise.

"Hey!" Ryan shouted. "What's that?"

"What?" Ling asked, walking toward him.

Another bamboo shoot began to wiggle. Ryan pointed to it. "That."

The cub tensed again. Then he pounced on the shoot.

Shhhhwip! It dropped out of sight. The cub fell on his face.

Ling chuckled. "Bamboo rat. It makes a tunnel underground. It steals the bamboo."

Another wiggle. The cub jumped again. He landed flat on his face.

Ryan and Ling couldn't help laughing. Chu took out his bottle and gulped down some more of the brownish liquid.

With a burp, he held the bottle out to Ryan.

Ryan took one look at the thick, mud-colored, gummy liquid and gagged. "I'll pass."

But Chu pushed it into his hands, urging him to drink.

"No, really," Ryan insisted.

Chu said something to him in Chinese.

"Grandfather says you have to drink something," Ling interpreted. "Besides, he gets insulted if you do not share a drink with him."

Ryan gulped. His throat was dry. He had barely eaten all day. His stomach was beginning to scream at him. At this point, even the bamboo was starting to look tasty.

How bad could the liquid be? So he had to share it with the old man — he'd shared chocolate with Johnny Pratt back home a million times.

Be brave, he told himself. *It's better than being thirsty*.

Ryan reached out tentatively. Then, summoning up all his courage, he grabbed the bottle, put it to his lips, and took a swig.

It didn't taste at all the way he'd expected.

It was much worse. Factory sludge, toxic

waste — *those* were things that came to mind. He nearly barfed.

"This is truly gross," Ryan said.

Chu replied in Chinese.

"Grandfather says it is good for you," Ling translated. "It will grow hair between your toes."

Chu continued. This time, Ling began to blush and shook her head.

Chu nudged her, urging her to speak.

"Grandfather says some women like hair between the toes," Ling said timidly.

Ryan tried not to crack up. Chu smiled slyly at him and winked.

Ryan winked back.

A few miles away, Po loped through the forest. His clothes, which he hadn't changed in days, were ragged and dirty. His face was shadowy with beard stubble. Over one shoulder was slung a heavy rifle. Over the other, two dead rabbits.

He stopped. Overhead, the distant, stuttering sound of a helicopter began, quickly growing louder.

Po squinted as he looked into a bright opening between the treetops. He waited until the chopper flew into sight.

When he spotted the panda symbol, he started to run.

The cave was nearby, but his partner had left his lookout post. "Shong!" Po called out.

No reply. The lazy halfwit must have fallen asleep. Po ran inside the cave.

Shong was sprawled on the floor, just inside the opening. He groaned, struggling to sit up.

"What happened?" Po demanded. "What are you doing?"

An attacker. The thought flashed through Po's mind. He scanned the cave suspiciously.

He stopped when he caught sight of the basket — on its side, unroped, empty.

Now Shong was on his feet. Holding his aching stomach, he gaped at the basket in anger. "The Western boy," he grumbled in Chinese. "He took the cub!"

"What did he look like?" Po demanded.

Shong held out his hand, indicating Ryan's height. "He couldn't have gotten very far."

Po was boiling. Did this "Western boy" take anything else? He stepped to the rear of the cave, then suddenly stopped.

Lying on the floor, almost hidden in shadow, was an unusual cap.

A baseball cap, with the symbol of an American team on it.

Po picked it up and examined it carefully. He had seen it before. It belonged to the American boy.

Chapter 14

When he heard the helicopter, Ryan leaped off his stone perch and looked frantically around for an open area. "We have to get out in the open so he'll see us!"

He, Ling, and Chu scrambled through the surrounding area. The trees were packed together. Their branches formed thick canopies, blocking all but specks of light.

"He won't see us down here!" Ryan exclaimed.

They fanned out, weaving through the thicket of trees. The helicopter's noise was receding sharply into the distance. "They're going to leave!" Ryan cried.

He stopped in his tracks, gasping for breath. Above him, a shaft of light beamed into his tired, hopeless face.

Ryan looked up into a patch of bright blue emptiness.

High above the forest, Lei steered the helicopter in slow circles. Chang and Richard peered intently out the window, examining the spaces between the trees for signs of life.

Before long, Chang passed over the clearing in which they had found Chih the day before. They had seen the clearing three times already that day, and Richard still held on to a faint hope his son might return.

"Let's land and find our equipment," he suggested. "Maybe they went back there."

Lei brought the helicopter down into the clearing. The sprung trap was still lying there, untouched since the previous day. But Richard could see no other signs of life.

He grunted as he used his cane to help himself out of the helicopter. He limped around the clearing until he found a small, barely trodden path. He had used this path with Ryan, Ling, and Chu. The equipment should be at the end of it, near the road he'd taken with his tractor.

"Come on," he called over his shoulder.

With his cane, the going was slow. Chang and Lei ran ahead of him.

Richard found them examining the equipment, exactly where it had been left. But the equipment was not the most important thing on his mind.

"Where the heck *are* they?" he said.

"We will look in the area. They cannot be too far," Lei reassured him.

Chang held the tracking antenna above him, slowly swinging it around.

"Are you picking up anything?" Richard asked.

The two other men spoke briefly in Chinese. Then Lei said to Richard, "No. The collar is not sending out a signal."

Ryan trudged through the thick undergrowth, following Chu. Beside him, Ling held the cub.

Before long, Ryan spotted light ahead. As the three approached it, he could hear the familiar rushing sound of water.

They walked out onto the bank of the canyon. The sagging bridge spanned the river, its walkway like a piano with broken and missing wooden keys.

"Not this again!" Ryan groaned.

"Is the American boy afraid?" Ling said with a smirk.

"No!" Ryan retorted. "I'm just . . . afraid for *Chu*. He might get hurt, being an old man and all."

A distant shout interrupted the conversation.

Ryan and Ling turned to see Chu on the other side of the bridge, signaling them to follow.

Ryan winced. So much for that excuse.

"Come on," Ling urged. "We must cross the bridge to get back to our equipment."

Turning her back to him, Ling began walking across the bridge, cradling the cub.

Ryan steeled himself. He had no choice now. He'd done it before, and he'd just have to do it again.

Wrapping his fingers firmly around the wire support, he stepped onto the bridge.

"Don't look down," he said under his breath. *"Don't look down."*

Two steps . . . three . . . four . . . five . . .

Ryan smiled. "Hey, this isn't so bad," he said.

He let go of the support. Grinning, he called out, "Look, Ling, no hands!"

Ling was halfway across. She turned, an annoyed expression on her face.

Looking at Ryan, she blanched. "Run!" she screamed.

Ryan was startled, but only for a moment. Ling was *not* going to get the best of him. No way. "Nice try," he said, "but I'm not buying it this time."

Crrrrrrack!

A bullet whizzed by his right ear.

"YEEEAAAAAAAGH!" A scream tore up through Ryan's throat. He grabbed the wire support and ran.

Ahead of him, Ling stumbled. Her foot slipped through a gap between wooden planks. The cub flew out of her flailing arms, landing on one of the planks.

Ling fell through the bottom of the bridge. Ryan watched in horror as her arms reached for a wire support along the bridge's bottom.

"Ling!" Ryan cried.

Her fingers closed around the wire. They held fast.

Ling swung high over the river, dangling.

Ryan ran up to where she'd fallen. He could feel the bridge rumbling. The poachers were sprinting toward them, but he had no time to look.

He reached down, trying to grab Ling's arm.

On the opposite bank, Chu ran out of a thick tangle of bushes. He sped toward the bridge.

Gritting his teeth, Shong raised his rifle.

Crrrrrrack!

Chu dived onto the bridge, hitting the boards with a sharp smack.

"Help!" Ling shrieked.

"Grab my hand!" Ryan said.

Ling reached for him, but she was too far away. Ryan needed to push himself closer. Lying on his stomach, he held tight to the bridge with one hand. He groped with his feet, trying to find a secure foothold.

Snap! Snap! Snap!

The rotted planks were giving way. They tumbled to the water as Ryan knocked them loose.

There. Ryan found a strong plank, planted himself, and clutched Ling's hand.

Behind Ryan, the poachers came running. Chu picked himself up and stormed toward his granddaughter.

Ryan pulled. Ling was small, but from this position she felt heavy as a truck. Ryan pulled as hard as he could.

Out of the corner of his eye, Ryan spotted the cub. The panda was jittery with panic. He skittered from one side to the other, afraid of the approaching enemies.

Finally, seeing no other choice, the cub jumped on Ryan's back.

Ryan lurched downward. "Hey!" he cried out, loosening his grip on Ling.

"Don't let go!" Ling screamed. "I can't swim!"

"I promise," Ryan vowed. "I won't let go!"

Adjusting his weight, Ryan dug his feet into the wire support. Again he pulled Ling upward.

Beneath Ryan's feet, two planks broke loose and fell. The poachers were now inches away. The cub clasped his arms tightly around Ryan's neck.

Ryan was choking. He hung to the support by the muscles of his toes. He gritted his teeth. His eyes saw red. He could not let go of Ling. He could not . . .

And he didn't.

His toes gave way. Ryan felt them unlock from the bridge. He could not hear himself scream. But he could feel the panda on his back. And he could see the water rushing toward him.

And he could feel the viselike grip of Ling's hand on his own as they plunged together.

Chapter 15

"Chu!"

Richard spotted the old man atop a hill, gazing downward. With Chang and Lei's help, Richard limped up to meet him.

Below them the river raged, a long, blue-black ribbon between the walls of the canyon.

Chu turned. His face was drawn and ashen, his eyes glassy. He said nothing.

Richard felt his skin prickle with fear. "Where are they?" he demanded. "What happened?"

Richard knew Chu. He was a talker. You asked him a question, he gave you a sermon. But now, when the old man opened his mouth, he could only moan one word, over and over.

Richard knew enough Chinese to recognize it. "The river?" he asked. *"The river?"*

Chu nodded, his eyes growing red.

Richard felt as if he'd been punched in the stomach. He looked over the hill and saw the bridge. It sagged like the rotting skeleton of a long, monstrous serpent. In the center, wires sagged among jagged, broken wooden planks. Below it, the water cascaded downhill for what looked like miles, breaking into angry white swirls around rocks and boulders.

Along the riverbanks Richard saw no signs of life.

Further downstream, over a steep crest of the river's descent, Ryan's head bobbed above the surface. His eyes strained to see where he was.

He was being borne along on the current. The river was a water slide, roaring furiously, smashing against rocks and tree stumps.

Ryan flailed his arms, fighting for control. Whitecaps slapped his face. The current twisted him downriver, smashing his body against rocks.

Ryan caught a glimpse of the panda cub's black-and-white fur, being battered along by the current. But where was Ling? He couldn't see her.

In a moment, he was pulled under, and everything went black.

Along the opposite bank, Ling tumbled along with the rough, coursing water. The riverbank sped by, a green-brown blur, dangerously close.

She cried out as she smacked painfully against a protruding root. Reaching out, she grasped on to it.

She held on and pulled herself to the shore.

Gasping for breath, she collapsed onto the grass. Everything seemed to be swirling. She blinked, rubbing her eyes, struggling to stay conscious. Her clothes were ripped and soggy, her backpack gone.

Ling fixed her gaze up the river. The bridge was out of sight. Ryan and the cub were nowhere to be seen.

"Ryan!" Ling called out. *"Ryan!"*

* * *

Her cries echoed against the canyon walls. Upstream, Richard was at the base of the hill now, searching the riverbank with Chang, Lei, and Chu.

At the faint sound, Richard paused. He hushed the others.

"Did you hear that?" he asked.

They all listened carefully, but the noise of the rushing water muffled all other sounds.

Discouraged, Richard shook his head. "I thought it was Ling."

Chu began wringing his hands. Words spilled out of him in a kind of desperate moan.

"What did he say?" Richard asked.

Lei looked uncomfortable. "Nothing."

But Chu was carrying on, practically in tears.

"What's he saying?" Richard demanded.

Lei hesitated, his eyes cast toward the ground.

"Tell me what he's saying!" Richard insisted.

When Lei spoke, his voice was soft and agonized. "He does not think the children survived the fall."

*   *   *

Ryan's eyes opened. He coughed, releasing a mouthful of water. He braced himself for another wrench of his body, another drop into the cold underwater blackness.

But he wasn't moving. He was *on* something. Solid. Soft.

He sat up. The soil beneath him was muddy from his soaking-wet clothes. His body ached with cuts and bruises. Inches away, the river flowed noisily.

Had he been pulled out? He looked around.

A furry panda face was staring at him, cocked curiously.

It was the cub. The cute, fluffy cub that nearly cost him his life.

"Take a hike," Ryan muttered.

Just beyond the panda, Ryan spotted Ling's backpack, lying on the ground.

He reached over and picked it up. It was waterlogged and half-unzipped. He looked around for signs of Ling, but she wasn't there.

Ryan was *starving*. He reached into the backpack and rummaged through. Ling had to have some beef jerky left. That would really hit the spot.

Ryan tossed aside the useless contents — soggy tissues, plastic pens, an old collar. Where was the beef?

"Ryan!"

Ryan jumped. It was Ling's voice. He never thought he'd be so happy to hear it.

Ling was beaming as she ran down the riverbank toward him.

Ryan fought the urge to run and greet her. Instead he nodded to her, then gestured toward the panda.

"Ryan, are you all right?" she asked.

"Yes," Ryan replied.

Suddenly Ling's smile disappeared. "You let me go!" she snapped. "I told you I cannot swim. I almost drowned!"

She grabbed the backpack out of his hands and pulled out some more tissues and a wet candy bar. "The meat sticks are gone," she said with a sigh. "All that is left is a candy bar."

"Split it with you?" Ryan asked.

"No, we must save it for an emergency."

"*This* is an emergency!"

The cub waddled up to Ling and sniffed the candy.

"The cub is hungry, too," she said.

"Hey, I got dibs on it!" Ryan proclaimed.

"The cub does not eat candy," Ling explained.

"So, how are we going to get back?"

Ling looked up the sloping river. "I am not sure how far downriver we came. If we can find Siguniang, we are okay."

"Siguniang?"

"It means, 'Four Sisters.' "

Ling scanned the surrounding area for a familiar sign. Her eyes stopped at something in the grass by a tree.

She ran over and picked up the radio collar.

"What's that?" Ryan asked.

Ling's eyes were wide with excitement. She answered him in her native language.

"English, please," Ryan reminded her.

"This is a radio collar," Ling replied, "to track the panda!"

She sat down, shaking the collar, smacking it. Finally she held it to her ear and rattled it. "The battery is loose."

As she dug her fingernails into the side of the battery compartment, Ryan grabbed the collar from her. "Let me try."

"No, *I* will!"

Ryan ignored her. He fiddled with the

collar, trying to pry off the compartment lid.

"You do not know what to do," Ling said.

"Relax," Ryan shot back. "I'm an American. My life revolves around electronics. I think I can handle it."

Click!

The compartment sprang open. Out popped the battery, high into the air.

Ling and Ryan could only watch as it sank into the river and disappeared.

"Did *I* do that?" Ryan asked sheepishly.

Ling was red with fury. "*You are a moron!* I will not talk to you," Ling snapped. "Now they will not be able to find us!"

Ryan smirked. "What makes you so sure they're looking for us in the first place?"

"*Of course* they are looking!" Ling glared at him, stunned. "My grandfather will be very upset."

"At least *somebody* will care."

"You think Grandfather would abandon me?" Ling asked. "You think Dr. Tyler would abandon you?"

"It wouldn't be the first time," Ryan said with a snort.

"You do not know what you are talking about. Your father is a good friend to the people here. A good friend to the panda."

Ryan's feelings gushed out. "That's the problem. He was too busy being everyone's friend — everyone but mine! I mean, why wasn't he in the stands when I was playing Little League and hit that triple? Why didn't he come to the emergency room when I broke my arm? Why didn't he come to Career Day with all the other fathers?"

Ryan's eyes misted over. He hadn't meant to tell Ling his life story. He hadn't wanted to show his weakness. But now here he was, on the verge of crying, stranded in the middle of nowhere, lucky to be alive — all because of his dad. How was he *supposed* to feel?

He choked back a sob. The last thing he needed now was Ling's pity. Turning away from her, he said, "Let's just get out of here, okay?"

Ryan hooked the collar onto his belt. Then he knelt to pick up the tossed-aside contents of the backpack. Behind him, Ling asked, "How is your batting average?"

Ryan turned. "What?"

"Your batting average?"

"Two fifty — but the season just started."

Ling nodded, impressed. "Much better than last year."

Huh?

She was right. It *was* much better. Ryan stood up, amazed.

"Your father read me your letters," Ling said with a shrug. "He read *everyone* your letters. He is so proud of you."

Ryan looked away. In his mind, his father hadn't even read the letters himself. Hearing Ling's words was like discovering the moon was made of candy.

He had a hard time believing it. But boy, did he *want* to.

The sun was beginning to set on Richard and his three colleagues as they walked down the riverbank. Chang led them, holding the tracking antenna. He mumbled something to Lei in Chinese.

Richard looked at Lei hopefully. "Is it picking up anything?"

Lei shook his head. "No. No signal."

"But I *know* Ling had the radio collar on

her," Richard replied. "She took it off Chih."

Chu spoke in a worried voice, looking up to the sky.

"Chu is right," Lei said. "The sun sets. We must come back tomorrow morning."

"I can't leave," Richard asserted. "Not until I find them."

"I understand," Lei replied, "but it will not do any good at night. No flashlight. No food."

"But I can't go back knowing they're —"

Lei cut Richard off. "There is nothing we can do now. Not till morning. First thing in the morning, we will come back."

Richard fell silent. He refused to believe the worst. Ryan *was* alive. He was out there, somewhere.

After the fall from the bridge, who knew what condition he'd be in? He might need immediate medical care.

And even if not, how safe would he be in the forest at night? He'd done it once, but now he'd be wet and battered — and *wanted* by two gun-crazy poachers, according to Chu.

Richard's heart refused to let him leave.

But as the forest became shrouded with darkness, his mind took over.

With mounting dread, Richard realized Lei was right. The search would have to be called off for the night.

He hoped he wouldn't live to regret it.

Chapter 16

As the helicopter set down in front of the panda reserve, Richard was glum and distracted. Wordlessly he climbed out and hobbled toward the front door.

Ryan was on his mind. His son had changed so much in two years — two years that had seemed to fly by in China.

Richard had never questioned his work. Preserving an endangered species had seemed so desperately important. Now he wasn't so sure. All Ryan's triumphs and setbacks, fights and celebrations, questions and discoveries — he'd missed them all.

Had it been the right thing to do? Had it been worth it if Ryan were now —

He couldn't finish the thought. He wouldn't allow himself to.

The last thing he wanted to do was lose hope. He had to take his mind off Ryan. Ryan was a big boy. He was with Ling. He'd survive.

The best thing to do was concentrate on something else. On work. Check up on Chih, whom he hadn't seen since the morning.

He walked straight to the hospital area. By now, he figured, Chih would be feeling quite a bit better.

But the room was empty.

"Chih," he said under his breath.

He rushed outside into the gathering darkness. Rounding the corner to the outdoor panda enclosure, he stopped. Two workers were carrying Chih on a thick wooden plank. She lay motionless, her eyes half-lidded.

The workers took Chih inside her cage and set her down. Then they left, throwing shut the gate.

Richard walked over to the cage and looked through the bars. Chih was sitting up now, staring into space.

"Hi, girl," Richard greeted her.

Chih kept staring, as if she hadn't heard him.

One of the workers returned, with a wheelbarrow full of bamboo. Opening the gate, he handed a few of the sticks to Chih.

She looked at them briefly, then turned away.

The worker kept nudging her gently with the bamboo, but Chih paid no attention. With a grunt of frustration, he gave up and walked away.

"Not eating?" Richard asked.

He sat down by the cage and looked at Chih's face. Pandas were funny. They were not capable of facial expression — or so the experts said — and yet somehow their features revealed so much.

Chih, Richard knew, was depressed. Despairing. Heartbroken without her young cub.

He knew just how she felt.

Picking up a piece of bamboo, he lifted it gently near her mouth. "You have to be strong for your cub when he comes back," he said.

Chih turned away again.

Chang emerged from the reserve kitchen, holding a bowl of steaming rice. He spoke in Chinese, but Richard recognized the sentence that meant "you must eat."

"Thanks," he said, taking the bowl.

But even though Richard hadn't eaten all day, the rice had about as much appeal as shredded plastic. He set it down on the ground.

"Guess I'm not hungry either," he said, smiling at Chih.

A light rain began to fall. Chih stood, looking into the muted light of the moon. As the drops pattered on the top of her cage, she began to bark.

Richard had never heard such longing and sadness in the cry of a panda. Her sound grew louder and louder, and soon Richard could hear an echo.

No, not an echo. An *answer*. From the surrounding forest came another panda's bark, and then a third and fourth.

Chih looked possessed, as if calling across the world. And in response, the forest seemed to be coming alive.

Richard could only sit back and listen, spellbound.

The barking made its way into the woods, deeper and deeper, as more pandas picked up the cry. It reached to the tree-tops, waking the monkeys. It caused the moles in the ground to take notice.

And in the hollow of an old tree trunk, sheltered from the rain, Chih's cub listened.

He stood up between Ryan and Ling. Rearing his little head back, he yapped loudly.

"He sounds like he's crying," Ryan remarked.

"According to my grandfather, panda bears cry," Ling said. "Want to hear the story?"

Ryan shrugged. "Go ahead. It's not like I'm going to go in the next room and watch TV."

Ling picked up the cub and cradled it while she spoke. "A long time ago, the panda bear was all white. The all-white panda had a friend, a young girl. She was the youngest of four sisters. The panda helped the girl as she herded her father's sheep. The panda and the girl were the best of friends. One day, a hungry leopard came. It wanted the panda. The girl tried to stop the attack. Instead of the panda, the leopard killed the girl."

The panda, all white? *Puh-leeze*. Ryan listened, for lack of anything else to do — but this was sounding pretty hokey.

"The girl's three sisters held a funeral by the river," Ling went on. "The pandas came from every part of China. In honor of the girl, all the pandas rubbed black ash on their arms. It was a sign of mourning. Very sad. The pandas all began to weep. They hugged each other to share in the sorrow. Black ash got on their white fur. They cried so much. All the pandas rubbed tears from their eyes. When the pandas opened their eyes again, the three sisters were gone."

"They bailed?" Ryan asked.

Ling shook her head. "The three sisters missed their sister so much, they jumped in the river. The sisters then joined hands at the bottom of the river. Next day, a mountain rose up with four peaks!"

"I bet that's the Four Sisters."

"Yes. They stand guard over the pandas, watch over them, protect them forever. And, so they would never forget the girl who cared so much, the pandas remained as they were. Black and white."

Ling's voice was a soft hush as she finished. She looked down at the panda cub, her eyes moist.

Ryan thought about it a moment. "That's a bunch of bull."

"My grandfather does not lie!"

"Then if these four sisters are real, how come the panda bear's going extinct?"

Ling turned away. She had no answer for that.

Not far away, Shong and Po came upon a patch of trodden-down grass by the riverbank. Nearby were some old wadded-up tissues.

They turned to each other and smiled. Bingo.

Holding a flashlight ahead of them, they quietly followed the trail.

As night fell, Ryan and Ling found a rotted-out tree trunk for shelter. Ryan was exhausted, achy, and starving. The trunk quickly became cramped and hot, and worst of all, smelly. He squirmed to find a comfortable position, but his body kept telling him, *Uh-uh, tried this already.*

"We are lucky we found the tree," Ling said.

"No," Ryan retorted. "*Lucky* would be finding a hotel with MTV."

He twisted around one more time, banging his head. "Ouch! *Man!*" With a frustrated groan, he blurted out, "I'd do anything right now for a Big Mac and fries and a chocolate shake and then a hot fudge sundae with nuts!" An idea struck him. "Hey, where's the candy bar?"

"No," Ling replied. "We must save it."

"For *what*? I'm hungry, I'm tired, I'm soaking wet, and I'm freezing!"

"But we saved the cub."

"Big deal!"

"You think the world revolves around you," Ling accused him. "You don't care about the panda!"

"If those poachers had shot the cub on the bridge today, we wouldn't be sitting in a tree right now."

"The poachers did not shoot at the cub. They shot at us!"

Ryan wasn't sure he'd heard that right. "They were shooting at *us*?"

"Yes," Ling answered.

"They can't shoot us. We're just kids!"

"There is a strict law in China. If you kill a panda, the punishment is very severe."

"How severe?"

"The punishment is death."

Ryan felt his whole body clench. "That's severe. I can't believe we're risking our lives for one stinking little bear!"

"The cub is very important. When the committee makes a decision on the reserve, they will vote to keep it open for another year if we have a healthy cub to show them."

"What do you mean?"

Ling yawned. Her eyelids were growing heavy with fatigue. "The committee will close the reserve down if we do not have a cub to show them."

"So if we get the cub back in time," Ryan said, "then the reserve'll have to stay open, and my dad will have to stay in China for *another year?*"

Ling's answer was slow, rhythmic breathing. She was fast asleep.

The cub, however, was wide awake. Hanging out near the opening, peeking outside. As if he were nervous to be around Ryan.

Which, considering the way Ryan was feeling, made perfect sense.

How could people get so worked up over

a little animal? It was cute, sure. And endangered. But was it worth *all this*? Risking the lives of two human kids? Separating a father and son?

And what would be Ryan's reward for returning the cub? Bye-bye, Dad. Enjoyed the trip, say hi to the murderers next time you see 'em.

No way. There had to be a way out of this.

Ryan yawned. It would have to wait until morning. He wasn't thinking straight.

He lowered himself to the ground and fell asleep.

The cub didn't move. He stayed in the shadows by the opening.

From outside came the sound of footsteps. The cub stood, stock-still, and watched two men pass by. One of them was holding a rifle.

Chapter 17

The morning sun was a shimmering globe of gold as Ryan climbed a grassy hillside. He had left the tree trunk while Ling was sleeping, and then carried the cub far into the forest, taking care to memorize his pathway from the tree shelter.

Ryan stopped by a bamboo patch. It was a perfect place to leave the cub. He would be nourished until some other panda found him.

Besides, the cub was getting heavy.

"Look, it's not my fault," Ryan explained as he set the cub down. "If I take you back to the reserve, then I won't be able to see my dad for another whole year."

The cub looked at Ryan, cocking his head to the side.

"You're better off here in the wild. I'm doing you a favor." Ryan picked a bamboo stalk and handed it to the cub. "Here's a little snack for the road. You can't follow me. You have to stay here. Go out and make some friends."

The cub looked at the bamboo stalk curiously. He turned the stalk over, examining it as if it were a toy.

When Ryan turned to walk away, the cub dropped the stalk and scampered after the boy.

"It's not a game," Ryan said. "Stay here."

He walked a few more feet. The cub paused for a moment, then followed.

"Go on! Get lost!" Ryan shouted.

The cub cringed. He looked up at Ryan, his dark eyes reflecting the sunlight. They were sad, *don't leave me* eyes.

Which was absolutely ridiculous. *Pandas do not have feelings like humans*! Ryan told himself.

He turned and ran, darting among the trees. When he was sure he was out of sight, he hid behind a wide trunk.

Catching his breath, he stood silently for a while. The cub hadn't followed him.

Ryan slowly peeked around the trunk. Through a thicket, he could see the cub.

He looked around forlornly for a moment. He took a few tentative steps.

Then, like a two-year-old boy, he dropped onto his behind and began to whimper.

Ryan felt a tug in his chest. The poor thing was so lonely. An orphan. "Don't do this to me," Ryan muttered.

The whimpering grew louder. "If something happens to this cub," Ryan said to himself, "I'll have to live with the guilt for the rest of my life."

Reluctantly he stepped away from the tree and walked toward the cub. "If you weren't so little and cute, this wouldn't be so hard," he called out. "I can't believe I'm talking to a bear."

The cub's ears perked up. He ran toward Ryan and jumped onto the boy's leg, hugging tightly.

Ryan tried to pry the cub off, but the little critter was *strong*. He took a few steps. The cub rode him.

"Have it your way," Ryan sighed.

He began walking back the way he'd come, and the panda swung along on his ankle.

Halfway to the hollowed-out tree, Ryan met up with Ling. Ling was relieved to see him, but angry that he had left — until she saw the panda on his leg.

"I think he likes you," she said with a laugh.

"I can't shake him," Ryan replied.

Ling suggested they should go toward the river and try to retrace their steps. Ryan agreed and let her lead the way.

He limped along with the panda, fighting back a smile.

They followed the sound of the water. They reached the riverbank at a shallow, sloping section, strewn with moss-covered rocks that poked above the surface.

Ling walked uphill, where the rocks were more numerous and closer together. "Look, we can cross the river here," she said.

As she knelt down to take the cub off Ryan's ankle, she noticed the radio collar attached to his belt. "Why do you have that?" she asked.

Ryan shrugged. "Because it might end up being my only souvenir from this trip."

The panda leaped happily into Ling's arms. She held it to her chest and carefully began stepping across the rocks.

Ryan put his foot gingerly on one of the stones. To his right, the river sloped far downhill. As far as he could see, the green, mossy rocks dotted the stream, looking like a convention of turtles.

Ryan almost fell into the water with his first step. He steadied himself on the thick, wet moss. "It's kind of slippery," he remarked.

Ling turned to answer. Her left foot landed on a rock and slid off. She windmilled her arms, dropping the panda cub.

Flailing, she grabbed hold of Ryan. Ryan braced his legs. His feet slipped out from under him.

"Who-o-o-oa!" Ryan, Ling, and the cub all landed with a splash. The current, coursing around the stones, carried them down the slope.

Ryan glanced over to Ling. She was bouncing on her rear, as if on a bumpy slide. The cub tumbled along beside her, its little body rolling along like a beach ball.

The stones were soft beneath Ryan. Once again he was being swept down the river. But what a difference. *This* ride was actually kind of fun! He burst out laughing.

Ling joined him. They hooted wildly, letting the stream carry them ever faster downward.

In the distance, Ryan heard a low, rumbling noise. He quickly shut up.

The noise grew into a roar.

"What's that noise?" he asked.

But before Ling could reply, Ryan saw where they were headed.

Directly toward a steep, foaming waterfall.

Chapter 18

"Oh, noooooooo!"

Ryan screamed. He tried scrambling toward the riverbank, clawing at the rocks.

His hands dug into the slime. Moss oozed between his fingers. The rocks battered him. He hurtled downward, ever faster, grabbing, kicking, fighting . . .

And then there was nothing. The river dropped out from beneath him, into a white cascade of water. He was flying, end over end. Ling and the cub shot out to one side. They all seemed to be suspended for a moment, and then they fell like lead weights.

This was it. He wished he could have said

good-bye to his mom, but it was too late now. Ryan braced himself for the end.

SSHHHHHHHHLURP!

Total blackness. Ryan couldn't breathe. He felt surrounded, suffocated. Was this what death was like? No wonder people tried to avoid it.

Maybe he could find a pocket of heavenly air, at least. He thrust his arms downward and felt himself rising.

With a gasp, he broke through a surface. He could breathe.

Breathe?

His eyes were gunked over with something. He wiped them off and looked around.

He wasn't dead. At least he didn't think so. Heaven couldn't have looked like this — a big pool of black slime at the bottom of a waterfall.

Ryan felt something move against his leg. He looked down to see a black creature rising from the muck, trying to attack his leg.

"Yeeeeagh!" Ryan jumped away, falling backward.

The slime monster shook its head, flinging away clods of gunk. Ryan got ready to bolt.

But he didn't. The creature was no monster. It was not even much of a threat.

It was the panda cub.

A sudden fit of giggles made him turn. Ling was a few feet away. Her face was caked with goop, in strange, dangly shapes.

"Ha-ha, very funny," Ryan said angrily. "If you want to see something funny, you should look at your face. There's stuff all over it."

"There is stuff on your face, too," Ling replied. She ran her fingers over some of the black mess. Much of it dripped off. But the long shapes held fast.

Ling's eyes suddenly grew wide. "Leeches!" she shrieked.

Ryan reached up to his face. They were hanging on him, too. He started hyperventilating.

Quickly the two of them began pulling. One by one, the leeches popped off with sucking noises.

They weren't just on Ryan's face, either. He could feel them under his shirt and pants, hanging on, sucking his blood.

Frantically he yanked and yanked, until

every one of them had fallen back into the muck.

When he was finished, he sighed with relief. But they were still covered with the slimy mud. Ryan glanced around. Not far from the muddy pool, the river ran deep and dark, fed by the waterfall.

As fast as he could, Ryan schlepped out of the muck. He ran for the water and dived in.

Moments later, when he surfaced, he could see Ling a few yards away, up to her neck in the water.

The cub scrambled onto the riverbank and watched, his eyes darting from Ling to Ryan.

Just out of earshot, the panda reserve helicopter swooped over the treetops, catching the rays of the blazing sun. Inside, the cabin was hot and sticky. Richard rubbed his bloodshot eyes and scanned the forest.

He and Lei had been looking for hours. Sunlight glinted off puddles left by the night's rainfall, and each flash of light had given them hope. But time and time again, they found nothing.

Lei glanced at his controls. "We have been out all morning," he said. "We must go back and refuel."

Richard did not answer. As the helicopter swung back toward the reserve, he stared silently out the window. More than ever, he regretted the two years he'd missed with his son.

Because now it looked as if he might never see him again.

Pale and grim, he turned away from the window.

He could not possibly see the two darkly dressed men directly below him.

Hiding under a thick, spreading tree, Shong and Po waited patiently for the helicopter to vanish from sight.

Chapter 19

"Ling, it's starting to get cold." Ryan tried to keep his teeth from chattering as they sat near the river. The sun had passed beyond the treetops, casting the river in afternoon shade.

"I'm not cold," Ling said, shaking.

"I can see you shivering from here," Ryan replied. "Why do you *do* that?"

"Do what?"

"Act like you're so tough."

"I *am* tough."

"Maybe. But you're allowed to have a little fun every once in a while."

"No time for fun. I am busy working with the pandas."

"But you're just a kid. Don't you ever want to go to the mall with your friends or play video games?"

Ling narrowed her eyes. "The . . . *mall?*"

"Yeah, it's a bunch of stores all together," Ryan explained.

"And this is fun?" Ling asked skeptically.

"Sure."

"Well, I have no time for friends. I must earn money to help my family."

"Why? Where's your dad?"

Ling looked away. "My father is dead."

"Oh." Ryan felt like a thoughtless fool. "I'm sorry."

"I have a mother and little sister in Chengdu. Dr. Tyler talked to the Chinese government so I could have a job in the reserve and be with my grandfather."

"*My* dad did that for you?"

"Yes. My mother is very happy because now she does not have to worry that I am without family. I am grateful to your father." Ling paused a moment, then gave Ryan a firm, level gaze. "You are very lucky to have a father."

Ryan had no answer. Whenever he

thought of his dad, *lucky* was about the last word that came to mind.

Now he was having second thoughts.

Richard pulled open the gate to Chih's cage. Walking inside, he held out a fresh stalk of bamboo.

The panda lifted her chin from the space between the bars. She glanced at Richard listlessly for a moment.

She took the bamboo and held it briefly, as if trying to decide what to do.

Finally she let it fall and stared dully through the bars.

Richard slid down against the cage wall and sat. The helicopter was having mechanical problems now. Any hope he had for a rescue was flying out the window.

Maybe Chih was sensing that.

"You must really hate us, huh?" he said.

Chih looked at him again.

"The bad guys take your cub from you," he continued, "and the good guys lock you up in this jail so you can't go out and find him. Makes no sense, does it?"

This looked ridiculous, talking to a panda. But Richard didn't much care at this point. He was tired of talking to people, and too depressed to be alone. "At least you did everything you could to show your cub how much you love him, Chih. Me, on the other hand . . . "

His voice trailed off as he thought back. Ryan's childhood seemed so distant, but scenes were popping into his mind like crazy.

"A few years ago," Richard went on, "Ryan and I went on this camping trip. Just the two of us. Ryan hooked a sixteen-inch bass. That fish was almost as heavy as he was. He fought that monster for half an hour. I thought he was going to quit a dozen times. I kept asking him if he wanted me to take over. 'No, Dad,' he kept saying. He wanted to do it himself. Well, he finally landed that fish and we laughed and hollered for an hour." Richard chuckled softly. "I'll tell you . . . my son, fighting that fish for so long . . . he was so *brave*. Certainly a lot braver than me."

The words caught in Richard's throat. He stopped talking and stared blankly at the ground.

"I'm a coward, Chih," he finally said. "I

put my work ahead of my family. Ahead of my *son*. And then I didn't have the guts to face him and own up to it. *That's* why I barely returned any of his letters. I didn't know what to tell him. I figured I'd talk to him in person when he came here." Tears began welling up in his eyes as he struggled with the words he had to say. "And I may never get the chance."

In the setting sun, Ling and Ryan still sat by the river. Now they were discussing Ryan's favorite topic, American TV.

"And they had all that clothing for just a three-hour tour?" Ling asked.

"Yep," Ryan replied.

"Did Gilligan and the castaways get rescued?"

"Yeah, but then they got stranded again."

Ling nodded solemnly. Then she looked Ryan straight in the eye. "You believe *this* and not the panda story?"

"Sure! It was on TV."

"Tell me the story of the bunch of Bradys."

BEEEEP!

Ryan grinned as he shut off his waterproof watch. *"American Gladiators,"* he explained.

His jaw dropped open. "My watch!" he cried. *"The battery!"*

He jumped up and unhooked the radio collar from his belt loop. "I can take the battery out of my watch and put it in the collar!"

Ling quickly got to her feet and they began to work on the transfer of the battery. Without a screwdriver it was not easy. Finally, using a sharp rock, they managed to pry open the watch casing.

Ryan took out the tiny battery and fit it into the radio collar.

Ling looked over his shoulder. "Careful," she warned.

"Got it!" Ryan exclaimed, snapping it into place.

Ling reached over and pressed a button on the collar. A red light flashed.

"It works!" Ling cried.

"Ryan," Ryan said, "you are a genius."

Chapter 20

At the panda reserve, Richard had fallen asleep next to Chih. He was awakened by Chang, shouting at him in Chinese.

Richard groaned as he opened his eyes. "What? What is it?"

Chang took Richard's arm and pulled him up. Then he ran out of the cage, signaling for Richard to hurry.

Richard grabbed his cane and followed. Chang led him to the tracking room and pointed to the electronic map. Shouting excitedly, he pointed to a flashing red light, indicating a section of the forest.

Richard leaned closer. His eyes brightened. "Ryan!" he said under his breath.

Chang ran out and returned with Lei. Together, Richard and Lei ran outside while Chang stayed by the tracking board.

The two men jumped into the old tractor and started the engine — but just as they pulled onto the road, a voice cried out in Chinese.

They skidded to a stop. Richard turned to see Chu running after them.

"He wants to go with you," Lei translated. "He says Ryan and Ling are his children, too."

Richard smiled. Chu scrambled into the tractor while Lei climbed out.

Ryan's feet ached. He and Ling had been walking for miles. By now that little cub felt like a lead weight. Ryan shifted it from one shoulder to the other.

Around them, the landscape had changed. The dense forest had given way to a mountain valley. Along the slopes, farms had been plowed into level terraces of land. Stalks of maize waved in the breeze.

For the last few minutes, the cub had been pretty still. He clung limply to Ryan, barely moving.

"Ling, do you think he's okay?" Ryan asked.

"He cannot go much longer without milk," Ling replied.

"Neither can we. I'm starved."

The cub began to squirm, kicking against Ryan's chest. Ryan carefully set him down.

The moment he hit the ground, he shot into the field.

"Come back here!" Ryan yelled.

The cub disappeared into the maize. Ryan and Ling tore after him, following the movement in the tops of the stalks.

Leaves slapped against Ryan's side. He lost sight of the cub and panicked. A moment later a flash of black and white appeared through the stalks. He sped ahead, trying to overtake the cub's path.

Stalks fell left and right. Ryan was gaining on the cub. Just a few more feet . . .

Ryan came to a sudden, dead stop.

In front of him was a man, standing in the middle of the field, dressed in a long robe and a turban. There was only one word to describe the look in his eyes.

Murderous.

Ryan's voice choked in his throat. "Ling?" he squeaked.

Beside him the stalks rustled. Ling emerged, looking frightened.

The man bellowed at them in an unfamiliar language.

"What's he saying?" Ryan asked.

"Can't tell," Ling replied. "He does not speak Chinese. He speaks Tibetan."

"Can't you understand him?"

"A little. I think he's mad."

"Thanks for the insight."

Behind them, the maize stalks crashed once again. The Tibetan man stopped shouting.

Out stumbled the panda cub. He stopped short, taking in the strange, tense scene.

Ryan thought the man was going to kill the little creature.

Ryan watched him closely, ready to bolt with the panda back through the maize. The man's face went blank for a moment.

Then, slowly, he smiled. He scooped up the panda and nuzzled him, laughing. Then he handed him to Ryan and gestured for him to follow.

After a long walk through the field, they approached a village.

It was like no place Ryan had ever seen

before. All he could do at first was gape. The villagers were dressed in colorful robes and turbans. Their small houses had walls of dried mud and thatched roofs. Beside each front door was a pile of chopped wood. The roads were made of packed dirt, and not a motorized vehicle was in sight.

A small boy, eating an ear of corn on a stick, stood next to his mother, gawking at Ryan. The moment Ryan looked at him, the boy ran behind his mother's dress.

A crowd gathered as the Tibetan man led Ryan and Ling into the heart of the village. They stopped before an extremely old man.

The guy made Chu look like a kid, Ryan thought. His skin was prunelike, his whiskers white and wispy. Although his eyes seemed almost closed, they seemed to penetrate deeply into Ryan, giving him the shivers.

Ryan looked nervously about. Everyone was staring at him, waiting stonily. Ryan felt as if he'd grown another head. What were they looking at?

The old dude must be some kind of village elder, Ryan figured. He bowed his head, feeling like a complete dork, and said, "How's it going?"

The village elder said nothing. Instead, he reached out for the cub.

Ryan pulled him back. No way was he going to let old leather-face get his creaky fingers on this bear. Who knew what he had in mind? Panda stew, maybe.

In a hoarse, crackly voice the village elder spoke in Tibetan.

"It is okay," Ling said. "He will not hurt him."

The old guy was grinning now. He did look pretty harmless. Reluctantly, Ryan handed the cub to him.

The village elder let out a kind of giggle. The other villagers began swarming around him, petting the cub, cooing happily.

Before Ryan knew it, he and Ling were sitting at a big table as the villagers ran madly around, preparing a meal. In no time, steaming bowls of food appeared in front of them.

Ryan had no idea what the stuff was. It looked a little like Chinese food, but he had never smelled anything so good in the States. He practically had to suck the drool back into his mouth. His stomach was jumping around, as if it wanted to reach out and grab the food itself.

Did you need manners in a place like this? Were you supposed to wait until everyone sat down? *What was this stuff, anyway?*

As the adults scurried around, the village children played with the cub, squealing with laughter. The Tibetan boy who had hidden behind his mother's clothes was now standing by Ryan's side. Ryan turned to him and smiled uncertainly.

The boy beamed.

"New friend," Ling commented.

Before long, the village adults were seated around the table. A woman poured a clear liquid into goblets for each guest.

Standing, the village elder raised his glass solemnly. Everyone at the table followed, including Ling.

Ryan gave her a curious look.

"Rice wine," she explained.

Feeling all eyes on him again, Ryan lifted his glass.

The village elder made a short speech in Tibetan.

"He who protects the panda is a friend of the village," Ling explained.

In unison, the villagers slugged back their drinks.

Ryan sniffed the wine. It didn't smell too strong. Not that he could really tell. He hadn't ever *tried* anything like this. No one else at the table seemed to be affected too much, though.

What harm could it do? he thought. Besides, *not* drinking it might insult the old guy.

Oh, well, bottoms up. Ryan gulped down the whole thing.

At first he thought he'd swallowed a knife. He felt as if he'd been ripped open from the esophagus to the stomach. He coughed. His face turned red.

Around him, villagers laughed and clapped him on the back.

Someone poured another round.

This time, though, Ryan was going straight for the grub. He felt around for a fork, but no such luck. By every plate was a pair of chopsticks and nothing else.

Ryan grabbed the sticks and dug into one of the dishes. He pulled upward, lifting a huge glob of food. But as he drew it toward himself, it fell to the table with a splat.

Across the table, two of the village women giggled.

The little boy, who now sat next to Ryan, was scooping piles of food onto his plate, no problem. Ryan studied him for a while and tried again.

Splursh.

Ryan's plate was still empty, but the table had some great-smelling food on it.

"Anyone have a fork?" Ryan called out.

He was answered by confused smiles.

Ling leaned over to him. She reached over his plate and took his hands in hers.

At her touch, Ryan felt very weird. He stayed calm on the outside. But his body shivered and he had an urge to blush.

Hunger pains, he told himself. *This is Ling, buddy*, he thought. *Not Lucy Sanders*.

"Keep this one still," Ling said, positioning one of the sticks in his hand. "Move this one only."

She helped his fingers manipulate the sticks. Then she let go.

Ryan was on his own now. The table fell silent. Everyone watched as he plunged the sticks into a pile of food.

147

Strong entry.

He carefully raised his arm.

Good lift.

Firmly, his fingers locked, he brought the food to his open mouth.

Score!

The food tasted even better than it looked. Ryan grinned from ear to ear.

A cheer went up from the table. The village elder toasted Ryan with another glass of wine.

Next to him, Ling was smiling. Ryan had never seen her so loose and happy.

"What is this stuff?" he asked.

"Monkey brain," Ling replied.

Ryan's jaw stopped working. He felt the blood draining from his face. "And *this*?" he asked, pointing to a plate of pinkish food.

"Steamed fungus in red chili, with pepper and fresh yak milk."

"*Fungus?* As in *athlete's foot?*" Without waiting for an answer, Ryan gestured toward a sweet-smelling brown dish. "Please say this is chocolate — "

"Slugs," Ling piped up.

Ryan set down his chopsticks. He felt the food sitting in his mouth with nowhere to go. He was feeling weaker by the second.

One by one, the villagers glanced at him. Their faces fell. They looked disappointed and worried.

They think they did something wrong, he thought.

Time to rally. It was Anti-Hurl Hour.

Chew, his brain commanded. Slowly his jaw began to move.

Swallow. Ryan hoped his stomach would not stage a coup.

The villagers smiled again, nodding proudly to one another. And Ryan's food stayed down.

Actually, if he didn't think about it, it wasn't half bad.

"I hate to break it to them," Ryan whispered to Ling, "but this isn't real Chinese food."

"Huh?" Ling mumbled, her cheeks bulging with food.

"Where are the egg rolls? Where's the wonton soup? I don't even see a fortune cookie."

Ling looked completely baffled as Ryan shoved in a steaming lump of fungus.

After dinner, Ryan felt stuffed and sleepy. In the soft glow of the setting sun, the adults cleaned up and the children played.

Ling held the cub in her arms. With her chopsticks she tried to feed him from a plate of food. But each time she did, the cub turned his head.

"Maybe there're too many people around, making him nervous," Ryan suggested.

The cub looked weak and limp. Ling's face was somber and sad as the village elder approached her.

He spoke to her briefly in Tibetan, and she nodded.

"We will sleep here tonight," Ling informed Ryan. "Tomorrow he will help us get the panda cub back to the reserve."

Many miles away, the panda reserve tractor puttered through the forest.

Richard's body lurched left and right. In the gathering darkness, it was harder to steer around all the ruts in the road. His injured leg banged against the stick shift, and he grimaced.

Behind him, Chu monitored the tracking equipment. Abruptly he looked up. He licked his finger, stuck it in the air, and screamed in Chinese: "*Stop!*"

Richard hit the brakes. The tractor swerved. The trailer fishtailed.

When it finally stopped, its wheels spun in the air.

Below them, dislodged rocks tumbled down a sheer cliff and disappeared into the darkness below.

Chu yanked out his bottle of brown liquid. He offered it to Richard.

Chapter 21

Ryan's eyes adjusted to the dark. Ling, the cub, and he were in a large, old barn. They were to spend the night there. Splintery wooden carts stood forlornly in the middle of the dirt floor. Against the wall were piles of wood and grain bins. Bulging potato sacks stood against a storage box filled with corn. A horse snorted lazily in his stall.

The village elder pointed up to the barn's loft. There, on a straw-covered floor, were more sacks of corn and potatoes.

The place smelled kind of moldy, but Ryan could deal with it. At this point, he could sleep anywhere.

Ling bowed to the village elder as he left.

Then she and Ryan walked to the ladder that led to the loft.

"After you," Ryan said.

Ling climbed upward. Ryan put the cub on a rung, then urged him up to the loft and followed close behind.

The straw was soft beneath Ryan's feet. "At least the accommodations are getting better," he remarked.

But Ling didn't answer. She was looking at the cub, who sat lifelessly against a sack. "Tomorrow may be too late." She sighed.

Ryan thought for a moment. There had to be an alternative to panda milk. If human babies could drink *cow's* milk . . .

That was it!

Ryan ran to the ladder. "Wait here!" he said.

He hurried down, then ran back to where the dinner had been. A few plates still sat on the table, along with the empty rice wine bottles.

With hand gestures, Ryan managed to tell some of the village women what he needed.

When he returned to the loft, the bottle was full of yak's milk.

He handed it to Ling. "It's milk from a

yak, so it's not exactly panda milk, but it might work."

Ling held the panda's head up. She raised the bottle to his lips.

The cub looked curious. His tongue darted out, tasting the whitish liquid.

Ryan's heart beat fast. Ling looked on hopefully.

The cub flinched, then turned his head away.

Ryan felt his whole body slump.

"It was a good idea," Ling said softly.

Minutes later, Ling was fast asleep. In the blackness of the night, Ryan listened to her regular, heavy breaths. Even though his body was weak with exhaustion, he couldn't sleep.

Silently he crept to the ladder and climbed down. In the dim starlight that filtered through the open door, he made his way outside.

The village houses were black lumps. Not one light burned. Ryan looked up into the sky. The stars blazed overhead, coating the sky with a pale white density he'd never seen at home.

He felt a furry object against his ankle.

Startled, he looked down and saw the panda cub's wide, white-patched eyes.

"Hi," Ryan said with a chuckle. "You know, we have to come up with a name for you."

He picked up the cub and pointed to the sky. "See all those stars? I know every constellation up there. My dad painted them on my bedroom ceiling. He said if I ever got lonely, I could look up at them and no matter where he was, we could be looking up at the same thing. That way we'd never be apart." He looked around for a familiar formation. "There's even one named after you. There it is, the Little Bear."

Ryan pointed to the Little Dipper. The cub's eyes followed his gesture.

"You're safe up in the sky," Ryan continued. "No poachers can get up there."

The sound of footsteps made Ryan spin around.

Ling was approaching. She smiled gently. "It is an old custom in China when a baby is born to bring the baby under the stars to give him a name," she said. "That way evil spirits will know he is from heaven. What name do you like?"

Ryan thought a moment. "He is a cub,

right? Why not name him after the best Cub that ever played major-league base-ball — Ernie Banks?"

"No, I do not like 'Ernie Banks' for a name," Ling said with a grimace. "How about a Chinese name — Ssu-ma Yang Hsuang-ju?"

Right.

Ryan didn't even bother attempting to repeat that. He knew he had to come up with something better — maybe a name that described the cub. *Black-and-white*? Nahh, that was stupid. *Roly-poly*? *Stubby*?

Then the perfect idea struck him. "I have a friend at home who's sort of short and fat," he said. "His name is Johnny. We could call the cub Johnny."

A smile spread across Ling's face. " 'Jah-Ni'? That is Chinese. It means 'best in the forest.' "

"Well, I doubt my friend Johnny is the best in the forest. Best in the lunchroom is more like it."

"I like the name. From now on the cub is Jah-Ni."

Ryan set Jah-Ni down. Now he was feel-ing homesick. And tired. "We better get some sleep," he said.

"Okay."

Ryan, Ling, and Jah-Ni walked back toward the barn. In the clear night air, Ryan felt he could almost taste the breeze. The distant maize stalks chattered with each cool gust, drowning out the song of the crickets and nightbirds.

Ling slowed to a stop. When Ryan turned to meet her glance, she looked away. "When you go to the mall," she said, her voice barely above a whisper, "I bet many girls like to go with you."

Dozens. Can't keep them away. They get angry at each other over me. I have to sneak there in disguise. Those were the words that popped into Ryan's head.

But he had no more energy for stories. "No," Ryan said, looking at the ground. "I'm not really a ladies' man."

"Oh. Maybe someday I will visit America, and you will take me to see the mall?"

When Ryan looked up, he saw a smile that looked exactly the way he felt inside.

The breeze blew through Ryan's and Ling's hair. It wound around the houses of the village, then picked up speed as it whipped through the maize field. Now a stiff, chilly wind, it barreled into the forest, bending the branches of the old trees.

As it gusted over the tractor that was parked aside an old dirt road, Dr. Tyler folded his arms across his chest.

He looked up into the starry sky and, for the first time in two days, felt a shiver of hope.

Chapter 22

In Ryan's dream, he was sitting before a huge, gooey sundae with hot fudge, caramel sauce, whipped cream, and seven maraschino cherries.

He was about to dig in when a hand covered his mouth.

Ryan sat up. He was awake now, and the hand was real. He cried out, but the sound gagged in his throat.

A Tibetan voice whispered into his ear, and Ryan looked up into the kind, craggy face of the village elder.

Ryan pulled the hand away. "What?" he asked.

The old man beckoned him to a window.

Ryan looked out and saw two grubby men storming through the village. Their clothes were unmistakable, and so was the rifle that one of them held.

Ryan ran to Ling and shook her awake. "The poachers are here!" he said into her ear.

Ling sprang from her straw mattress. When she glanced out the window, her face went pale. "They cannot see Jah-Ni!"

"How are we going to get out of here?" Ryan asked. He looked around frantically. They were trapped. The minute the poachers stepped in here, forget it. Hiding behind a sack would work for a while, but then what?

Ryan's eyes took in the entire barn — the sacks, the carts, the boxes . . .

"I have an idea!" he whispered.

The poachers were sweaty, tired, and bubbling with anger when they slid open the barn door.

Inside, the village elder loaded sacks of potatoes onto an ancient, wooden, horse-drawn cart. He looked up, unhurried, unfazed.

In Chinese, Shong demanded, "Have you

seen a young Western boy with a panda cub?"

The village elder understood Chinese, but answered in Tibetan, "I'm sorry, but I can't understand you."

Po stalked around the barn, pulling open sacks, snooping behind the grain bins, peering into dark corners and under carts.

Shong looked suspiciously at the sacks in the horse-drawn cart. He reached up to untie one of them.

The village elder's arm darted out. He grabbed Shong's wrist. Then, with his other hand, he pulled a potato out of another sack. Calmly, in Tibetan, he explained, "A potato."

Po, stomping toward them in disgust, yelled out in Chinese, "Let's go. They're not here!"

Shong was not so sure. He stood his ground, eyeing the cart.

The village elder stared at the poacher levelly.

Until he saw a moving object emerging from the shadows, behind the poachers' backs. It was a small sack, upside-down, walking on two furry black paws!

161

"I have work to do!" the old man blurted out in Tibetan.

He pushed the poachers out of the barn door, making sure to keep them facing away from Jah-Ni.

Grumbling, Shong and Po left the barn, with a vow to search the whole village.

The village elder muttered a joyful prayer. He walked over to Jah-Ni, who had almost wriggled out of the sack. Stuffing the cub back inside, the old man lifted it onto the cart.

He placed the cub next to the sacks that contained Ling and Ryan. Then he opened the stall and grabbed the reins of the horse.

In a few minutes the horse was hitched up to the cart, and the village elder led him slowly out the barn door.

As the cart made its way through the streets, the village children gathered around, walking alongside.

Ryan peeked out of his sack. The potatoes smelled something awful, and he wondered when he'd be safely out of sight.

Ling was still in her sack, tied up and snug. A few potatoes had fallen to the floor of the cart and were bouncing around.

Beside the cart, the village children were

laughing and singing. Over their heads, Ryan could see Shong and Po, running from building to building.

Oops. Time to make friends with the potatoes again.

As Ryan ducked back into the sack, he caught sight of Jah-Ni. The cub had escaped his sack and was climbing off the back of the cart.

One of the children screamed. The others gathered around, yelling at each other, trying to hide Jah-Ni.

Fat chance. The poachers heard the noise and stopped in their tracks.

In an instant, they were charging toward the cart at top speed!

Chapter 23

Ryan struggled out of his sack. Potatoes thudded to the wooden floor. He jumped off the cart and grabbed Jah-Ni from the children.

The poachers were gaining. "Move this thing!" Ryan shouted.

The village elder whacked the horse's rear end. With a snort, the horse picked up speed.

Ryan climbed onto the cart. Jah-Ni wanted nothing to do with it. He squirmed and tried to jump back toward the village children.

Ryan lost his balance. Below him, the rocky road whizzed by. With one hand he grasped a wooden slat. With the other, he yanked Jah-Ni back up into the cart.

The children ran full-speed behind the creaky wheels. The poachers were gaining on them, sprinting right by the village elder.

Next to Ryan, Ling's sack jerked furiously. "I cannot get out!" cried her muffled voice from inside.

Shong had pulled ahead of Po. He barged through the crowd of children. His face twisted with anger, he reached for the cart.

Beside him ran the boy who had taken a liking to Ryan. The boy stuck his foot in Shong's path.

With a sharp cry, Shong tripped. His fingers slapped against the cart as he tumbled to the ground.

Ryan held on tightly. The horse had broken into a gallop. The cart jounced violently over the rough roads, past the farm country and into the forest. Ryan felt his teeth crashing together. The horse's frayed leather harness creaked with each sudden tug.

"Untie me!" Ling yelled.

Ryan crawled to the sack and dug his fingers into the knot. "I'm trying!"

Don't force it, he told himself. He pushed and prodded until the rope loosened. Then he quickly yanked the two strands apart.

"Here!" he said, pulling open the sack.

Dazed, Ling climbed out.

Snnnnnap!

The harness broke. Its ragged remains flew into the air. The horse, freed from its burden, took off like a shot around a bend in the road.

The cart plunged straight ahead, into the forest. Ling screamed. Ryan held on to her and the cart for dear life.

With a sickening thud, the wheels hit a stump. The cart flew. It bounced away, flipping over twice.

When it finally stopped, it was upside down. Ryan caught his breath. His head ached and his sides felt bruised.

Pushing aside the piles of spilled potatoes, Ryan, Ling, and Jah-Ni crawled out into the dappled sunlight.

"Are you okay?" Ryan asked Ling.

"Yes," she replied.

Ryan looked at the cub, who was sitting by the cart. "Is Jah-Ni?"

"Yes. He is okay."

Ryan stood up. He glanced out toward

the road. No sound, no sign of the poachers.

Yet.

He turned the other way and let out a gasp.

Looming before them, under a halo of clouds, stood four tremendous mountain peaks.

"The Four Sisters," Ryan whispered. "Pretty cool."

Ling nodded.

Jan-Ni began coughing. The coughs quickly grew into wheezes.

"He sounds sicker," Ryan said, lifting the cub off the ground. "How far are we?"

"The reserve is on the other side of the mountain," Ling answered. "I'm afraid it will take a day to go around."

"We don't have a day. What if we took a shortcut and went *through* the mountains?"

"No. It is much too dangerous. The passages are very narrow. Very steep. There is much fog. Many people have gone through and were never seen again."

Jah-Ni coughed again. Ryan held up the cub's head and saw his glazed, bloodshot eyes.

"Ling, he's dying. We don't have a choice."

On a tree-covered hillside in the forest, Richard and Chu wound their way upward. Chu listened carefully through a headphone connected to the tracking antenna.

He stopped in his tracks. His face went slack and he ripped off the headphone.

"What is it?" Richard demanded.

Chu looked sick. He said something rapidly in Chinese.

"What?" Richard asked.

Chu repeated himself, slowly. Richard recognized the word *Siguniang*.

"The Four Sisters?"

Chu nodded sadly.

"Oh, no," Richard murmured. While the antenna picked up a moving signal, there was hope.

But no one made it out of those mountains alive.

Chapter 24

Lei greeted Chih with a smile as he walked into the panda enclosure. He carefully lifted her arm and examined her wrist.

Good. The sutures were healing well.

Now, if only they could work on her mood.

Lei had faith in Richard. If anyone could find the kids and the baby panda, he could.

The sound of an engine made him jump to his feet. This could be it! He patted Chih reassuringly and ran to the entrance of the panda reserve.

There he stopped short. It was not the tractor.

The government committee's minibus

trundled up to the curb. It groaned to a stop, disgorging a group of crabby-looking men in suits.

Judging from their faces, the men were not going to be patient and understanding. They were going to want results. It was either a panda cub, or bye-bye to the reserve.

Lei was gushing sweat.

Far from the reserve, Ryan led the way up a steep incline. Ling followed close behind, carrying Jah-Ni. Tendrils of thick fog wrapped around them. Ryan's clothes were soggy, and his heart knocked rapidly against his chest at the higher altitude. Through the soupy atmosphere, all he could see was the ground under his feet. He used a bamboo cane to steady himself as he climbed.

Stopping by a boulder, Ryan licked his index finger and held it high. It felt basically like a wet finger.

"Now, *how* does Chu do this?" he asked.

Behind him, Ling gasped for breath. She sat down on the ground. "Ryan, I cannot climb anymore. And the cub is so heavy."

Ryan knelt next to her. "Come on, Ling,

we can't give up now. It's not much further."

Ling set Jah-Ni down on a rock ledge. He slumped to one side, his eyes barely open.

"Ryan, it is no use," she said. "He cannot even hold his head up. We will never make it."

Ryan had never felt more alone. Ling and Jah-Ni were fading. But they couldn't retreat now. The poachers had tracked them as far as the village. They weren't about to stop. They'd find the cart. They'd realize Ryan and Ling could have gone only in one direction.

"Listen up, Ling," Ryan said. "Remember the bridge? Remember when I wouldn't let you go? Jah-Ni's not going to die. I'm not going to let him."

Ling looked up at him. Ryan could see something sparking behind the sadness in her eyes.

"I promise," he said firmly.

He stood up and held out his hand. Ling sat, motionless, her body as limp as the cub's.

Then, without a word, she reached toward him.

Ryan pulled her to her feet. She glanced anxiously at the cub, and Ryan knew what she was thinking. "Don't worry," he assured her, "I've got an idea how to carry him."

He removed Ling's backpack, adjusted the straps, and put it on himself. Then he asked Ling to lift Jah-Ni into it.

The cub felt like a major homework day, but Ryan could deal with that. They trudged slowly upward, into an ever-thickening mist. The path widened for a while, then became narrow enough for only one person. To one side, it dropped off sharply. Under the swirling fog, Ryan couldn't tell how *far* it dropped off.

Until they wound around a sharp bend, where a stiff wind had cleared much of the fog away.

Then Ryan could see all.

His stomach became a three-ring circus with a trapeze act.

Below them was a sheer cliff. Not far away, a waterfall thundered downward into a gorge that ran like a deep gash through the countryside. Distant fields stretched out endlessly in all directions, flat and green.

"Please, Four Sisters, don't let me fall," Ryan said under his breath. "I'm on your side."

He heard a sudden scrape behind him. Turning quickly, he saw Ling struggling for balance. A rock in her path was tumbling toward the edge. Ryan realized she'd tripped on it.

He grabbed her flailing arm until she was steady. "Careful," he warned.

The rock rolled off the pathway and out of sight. Ryan and Ling turned away from it and continued the climb.

Had they looked over, they would have seen the rock tumble down the cliff. They would have seen it bounce against a part of the switchback trail they had just covered.

And they would have spotted Shong and Po, dodging out of the rock's path.

Chapter 25

Chu knew the terrain. When he had suggested taking a path over the Four Sisters, *away* from the tracking signal, Richard had thought the old man was crazy.

But now Richard knew better. He and Chu were climbing the other side of the mountain from Ryan. The signal was getting stronger again. Stronger than ever. Now it was only a matter of time.

His leg had felt a lot better in the morning, but now it throbbed with each step. He was traveling light — a long rope wrapped around his belt, and a few tools — but even that was a burden. He gritted his teeth. Nothing could stop him now. He would reach the top even if his leg fell off.

He and Chu walked along a ledge, then wound their way around a sudden bend. The other side of the mountain came into view.

But Richard ignored the waterfall and the fields and the gorge. His eyes were drawn to the two poachers, scrambling up the pathway.

Where were the kids?

"Ryan!" he shouted. "Ling!"

His voice echoed, unanswered.

Richard's shout was lost in the thick fog around him. Hiking through that fog, shielded from Richard's sight, Ryan and Ling climbed steadily.

Ryan could see the mountain curve sharply. He followed the ledge upward until he could see around the curve.

"I can see the other side!" he shouted over his shoulder. "Hang on, Jah-Ni, it won't be long now!"

Ryan scampered around the corner, then came to a dead stop.

A scream tore up from within him.

"Why stop?" Ling asked as she walked up beside him.

Ryan did not need to answer. In front of him the ledge itself dropped off. Beyond it was nothing.

Ryan and Ling stood there in shock, looking at the valley miles below.

"It just . . . *ends*," was all Ryan could say. "There's nowhere to go."

"We must go back," Ling urged.

"But there's no time!"

Ryan looked up. He and Ling were standing against a rock face. High above them, a few branches peeked over the top of the rock. No help there. They were way out of reach. Ryan's eyes searched desperately for a handhold, a hidden path, a hiding place — anything.

Instead, he came face-to-face with Shong and Po.

Chapter 26

"*Ling!*" Ryan shouted.

Ling turned. A cry caught in her throat.

The poachers stood inches away, blocking the path. One step backward, and Ryan would be airborne.

"Stay away from us!" Ryan said. "I'm warning you!"

The poachers yelled at him in Chinese.

"He wants Jah-Ni," Ling translated.

"He's not getting him!" Ryan vowed.

Shong reached over Ryan's shoulder, toward the backpack.

"No!" Ryan angled his body away, but it was useless. He had no room to move.

As Shong lifted the cub easily out of the

pack, Ryan felt his blood boil. He watched Po leering greedily as he roughly took Jah-Ni out of Shong's hands.

That did it.

"Give him back!" Ryan yelled. Without thinking, he dived at the sniveling poacher.

Po fell to the ground with a startled grunt, holding tightly to Jah-Ni. Ryan straddled Po, pummeling as hard as he could, inches from the edge of the cliff.

Ling joined the fight, trying desperately to pull the cub away.

Shong stood over them. He reached down and grabbed Ling. With his other hand, he took the rifle from around his back.

Sounds of the struggle carried out over the abrupt end of the ledge. They snaked around the immense rock to its opposite side.

There, Richard and Chu were approaching the end of *their* ledge.

Both of them stopped at the noise.

"Ling!" Chu blurted out.

Richard looked over the steep edge. No climbing down there.

Then he spotted the branches hanging over the top of the boulder.

Quickly he unraveled the rope from his belt. One end of the rope was looped, and he made it into a lasso.

Swinging with all his strength, he tossed the rope upward. It caught on the thickest branch, and Richard yanked it tight.

Holding the rope with both hands, he climbed the smooth rock face. His injured leg felt a deep stab of pain, but he ignored it.

Richard stepped sideways, slowly traversing the rock.

On the other side, Shong pried Ling off Po. Ryan sprang to his feet and grabbed his bamboo cane. He jumped into batting stance and took a home-run uppercut — right into Po's left knee.

Thwockkk!

"Eeeeeyahhh!" Po cried out.

"Strike one," Ryan announced.

He drew the cane back and swung at the other knee.

Thwockkk!

"Strike two," Ryan said.

In agony, Po let go of Jah-Ni and fell to the ground. The cub rolled to the edge of the drop-off.

Ling ran for the cub. Shong grabbed her arm, pulling her back.

Spinning around, Ling swung with her other arm. She caught Shong's rifle in the middle of the barrel.

It flew out of his hand and over the ledge.

Shong's face turned bright red. His lips curled back over his teeth into a snarl of rage. With both hands, he dragged Ling to the edge.

"Ryan!" she screamed. *"Help!"*

"Ling!" Ryan dropped the cane. As he ran toward her, Po reached up and pulled him back by the shirt.

"Leave her alone!" Ryan cried, struggling to get loose.

Kicking and screaming, Ling grasped on to a tree root that jutted out of the ground. Shong peeled Ling's white-knuckled fingers off, one by one.

Ryan twisted and fought, but the poacher was stronger than he expected.

"Liiiiing!"

The shout came from above Ryan. He craned his neck upward.

Swinging by a rope across the rock, his eyes flaring, the veins of his neck bulging, was . . .

Indiana Jones?

Ryan blinked. *This is a dream*, he told himself.

But it wasn't. As the man swung closer, Ryan caught a good look at his face.

"Dad!" he cried out.

Shong looked up.

Smack! Richard planted his bad foot square in Shong's jaw.

The poacher lurched backward, away from Ling. He fell to the ground, headfirst, and lay there.

Ryan smiled. His dad had knocked Shong unconscious!

As Richard pulled Ling to her feet, Ryan looked around for Jah-Ni.

He spotted Po climbing up the steep mountainside, the cub squirming in his arms.

"He's getting away!" Ryan yelled.

He scrambled upward, grabbing on to trees for support.

Po slipped and slid, pulling himself up with one hand.

Ryan leaped. He grabbed hold of Po's

foot. Po tried to kick, holding fast to a scrawny tree trunk.

Ryan felt himself sliding. Now Po was his only support. He tightened his grip and yanked hard.

Po's fingers slipped. He let go of the tree and somersaulted downward.

Ryan hit the ledge first, on his side. Po crashed down after him. With a sickening thud, his head hit the rock. Po was out cold.

Jah-Ni flew out of his arms. Ryan watched with horror as the cub sailed over the ledge.

Chapter 27

"Jah-Ni!"

Ryan crawled to the edge and looked over.

A few feet below, a thick branch jutted out from the cliffside. Jah-Ni hung from its tip, legs swinging.

The cub glanced up at Ryan with wide eyes, whimpering loudly.

No time to think. Ryan jumped onto the branch.

Richard and Ling turned ghostly white. They ran to the ledge.

"Ryan, come back here!" his father commanded. "That branch can't support you!"

Ryan knew his father was right. What

he was doing was insane. The branch sagged with his weight. He was close enough to scramble up onto the ledge. If he were thinking straight, that's just what he would have done.

But all he could think of was Jah-Ni. All he could see was the little black-and-white furball dangling, crying, its last ounces of strength holding back death.

Ignoring his father's warning, Ryan stood up. The branch was thick enough for his feet, and walking would be the fastest way to reach Jah-Ni.

He stepped forward.

Creeeeeeeak. The branch dipped lower.

Ryan's knees buckled. He lifted his arms outward, balanced himself, and continued.

"Oh, no," he heard his father murmur.

"Ryan, *please.*" Ling sounded as if she were crying.

Left. Right. Left.

"Aagh!" Ryan's foot slid off the branch.

Instantly he shifted weight. He braced his knees and leaned the other way.

Balance again. Ryan checked Jah-Ni. The little guy was still hanging on.

Breathing deeply, Ryan edged closer.

"It's all right, Jah-Ni," he said. "I'm coming."

The branch groaned. Ryan stood still as he felt it droop.

When it stopped, he slid his feet forward. He was inches away now . . . inches . . . just about within reach . . .

Near the tip of the branch, Ryan carefully knelt.

"Hi, Jah-Ni," he said with a smile.

The little cub was hugging the branch now. Holding on with his legs, he reached out to Ryan.

Ryan could not move any farther. The branch was too narrow. But if he reached far enough, he could grab Jah-Ni's paw. He just knew it.

"Oh, Four Sisters, please help," Ling's voice pleaded.

Ryan leaned forward. He glanced at the countryside, which seemed miles below him. His stomach gave a quick, hard jump.

Steady, Ryan told himself. *Don't blow it now.*

The panda cub stretched his body. His arm seemed to elongate.

In front of Ryan, a hairline crack had

formed in the wood. If the branch broke off, Jah-Ni would be history.

Ryan's fingers were almost touching. It was going to work. *It was going to work!*

Then, with a sharp snap, the branch finally gave way.

Ryan lunged forward. He thrust out his arm, practically tearing it from its own socket.

As the tip of the branch fell away, he grasped Jah-Ni's fingertips.

He held tight.

Jah-Ni swung out. Ryan pulled the cub in and hugged the panda to his chest.

Jah-Ni clutched him as if he'd never let go. Ryan felt a drumming like a heavy rain on a rooftop. He wasn't sure if it was his heart or the cub's.

Over. It was over.

A warm tear trickled down Ryan's cheek. "I love you," he whispered.

Crrrrrrack!

The branch sank suddenly. Ryan felt as if he were on a dropping elevator.

"Ryan! Hurry!" Richard yelled.

Ryan needed no urging. He edged slowly back toward the cliff. Below him, a crack ran along the length of the branch.

Richard's arm reached far over the ledge. In his peripheral vision, Ryan could see Chu making his way across the huge rock, using the lasso.

Closer . . . Ryan moved slowly, avoiding any sudden motion. His dad's fingers were almost within reach, but not quite.

Closer . . .

"Ling!" Chu cried out, jumping onto the ledge. Ryan saw him wrap his arms around his granddaughter, shielding her eyes.

He doesn't want her to see me die. Ryan pushed aside the thought.

The branch was about to go. Ryan could feel it. He had no time to move nearer.

"Dad!"

The word left his mouth, half a plea, half a farewell.

He reached out across the hopelessly distant space.

At that moment, the branch gave way.

Chapter 28

Ryan closed his eyes. He held on to Jah-Ni, bracing for the plunge.

If they were to die, they'd do it together.

But he wasn't falling. He was hanging. Strong, viselike, *familiar* fingers were entwined around his own.

With a firm, steady pull, Richard lifted his son upward.

Ryan collapsed onto the ledge. Richard grabbed him by the shoulders. His face radiated a kind of insane mixture of rage and love.

"You could have been killed!" Richard bellowed, his voice about an octave higher than normal. "Are you okay?"

He didn't wait for an answer. Instead, he wrapped his son in a bear hug.

For a moment, Ryan wanted to freeze time. The hug brought back flashes of his childhood — all the best parts.

But there would be plenty of time for that later. His mission was not over yet.

"Jah-Ni's real sick, Dad," Ryan said. "We have to hurry."

Richard released his son. With a solemn nod, he ran over to the dangling rope and brought it toward Ryan.

Ryan had never imagined he could learn to scale a rock so quickly. But he did. And so did Ling.

Seeing Chu and his dad do it, each carrying a poacher on his shoulders, was truly awesome.

Even with the heavy load, they reached the tractor in no time. Richard strapped Shong and Po, still unconscious, onto the trailer.

Chu climbed into the driver's seat. Ryan, Ling, and Richard squeezed in next to him, holding Jah-Ni on their laps.

His index finger pointed straight up, Chu drove through the forest like a drag racer.

Ryan's bones rattled. He thought his teeth would crack into pieces. When Chu finally pulled onto a smooth village road, Ryan wanted to shout hallelujah.

Then, around a curve, a screech of brakes sent everyone shooting forward.

A herd of goats was crossing the road. Hearing the brake noise, the goats looked upward.

Then, definitely unimpressed, they continued their lazy journey.

Chu leaned on the horn. He screamed. He cursed a blue streak (well, Ryan *assumed* the words were curses). The goats were not amused.

Ryan looked at Jah-Ni. The brush with death had taken a lot out of the little cub, who now seemed barely conscious.

"We'll never make it!" Ryan said.

As the tractor waited, another contest of wills went on at the panda reserve. Lei served the committee members tea. He revealed the latest research. He showed them the stitchwork on Chih's wrist.

Finally Mr. Hsu whispered sharply to a committee member, who announced, "Mr. Hsu cannot wait any longer."

"Dr. Tyler will be here soon," Lei insisted.

"It no longer matters," the committee member replied. "You have no panda cub to show us."

As the committee turned to leave, Lei felt his hope — and his job — flying out the window.

Not to mention the hopes of the entire panda reserve.

Chapter 29

Chu's foot was pressed to the floor. The tractor barreled down the road. The panda reserve was in sight now.

As they squealed to a stop in front of it, Ling cried out, "The committee! They are leaving!"

Chu glanced over his shoulder. The mini-bus, crammed with dark-suited committee members, was pulling onto the road.

Chu stepped on the gas. He yanked the steering wheel toward the road again and drove directly in front of the bus.

EEEEEEEEE . . .

The bus swerved to avoid a collision. Chu

slammed on the brakes. Ling, Ryan, and Jah-ni went flying off.

Richard leaped out of the tractor as Mr. Hsu stormed off the bus.

"Dr. Tyler, what is the meaning of this?" the charcoal gray-suited official raged.

"I'm sorry," Richard began to explain, "but we couldn't let you go without — "

"It is too late," Mr. Hsu snapped. "The decision has been made to close the reserve."

Richard's face fell. "Close the reserve?"

"Yes. You have not been able to successfully breed here." Mr. Hsu began to turn away. "I'm sorry, even one cub . . ."

"But you don't understand!" Richard protested.

By now the committee members had filed out of the bus. But they had stopped scowling. One by one, their faces were lighting up with smiles.

Richard turned to see Ryan walking toward the entrance, holding Jah-Ni.

"Aaaah," one of the committee men cooed.

"Oooooh," said another.

"Oohhhh," chimed in some others.

Mr. Hsu stood still for a moment. As he watched Ryan disappear through the entrance, his men chattered like children.

With a wide grin, Mr. Hsu turned around and extended his hand. "Dr. Tyler," he said, "the reserve will stay open."

Richard returned his smile. He bowed gratefully and shook Mr. Hsu's hand. He took the news like a professional, calm and composed.

But inside, he was tap-dancing.

Ryan's heart sank as he and Ling approached the panda enclosure. Chih was curled on the ground, in the fetal position. Her eyes stared off blankly into space.

When Ryan pulled open the cage door, Chih did not move a muscle.

He set Jah-Ni down and gave a gentle push. The cub waddled uncertainly toward its mother and stopped.

Chih raised her head. Her eyes locked on Jah-Ni.

For a moment, she said nothing. Then a hoarse whimper welled up from inside her. She pulled herself up on to all fours.

Chih's injured paw was heavily bandaged. She seemed to wince as she limped toward her waiting cub.

All around them, the other pandas were walking to the bars of their cages. A few of them nodded excitedly.

Jah-Ni began to quiver. He held out his little paws.

With a strong sweep of her arms, Chih pulled the little cub tightly to her chest. For a moment the patches of his fur seemed to melt into hers.

Then, without wasting any precious time, Chih did the one thing she knew was necessary. She began to feed her starving cub.

Ryan sensed Ling walking up beside him. He didn't care if she noticed he was crying.

She wasn't in such great shape either.

Chapter 30

Ryan watched intently. His dad had once told him that panda cubs could be very fragile. Jah-Ni was slurping away but still seemed weak and sickly.

Ryan hoped this whole crazy adventure hadn't all been in vain.

Chu was now whispering something to Ling. He pushed her toward Ryan, urging her to say something.

"My grandfather wants to thank you for keeping his granddaughter safe," Ling said. "And the panda."

Ryan looked the old man in the eye. "You're welcome."

Chu smiled and bowed.

A question still nagged Ryan. He licked his finger and held it in the air. "Ling, ask him how he can tell things by his finger."

Before Ling could say a word, Chu burst out laughing. He leaned close to Ryan and whispered in his ear. Ling strained to listen.

"*What?*" Ryan said.

Ling smiled. "He says it is a very simple explanation: 'I lick my finger, then it becomes wet. So I must hold it up in the air to dry.'"

Ryan raised a skeptical eyebrow. Chu cackled at the reaction and walked away.

Ling quickly kissed Ryan on the cheek. "You are very brave, like your father."

Whoa. Ryan had not expected that. He felt his face heating up. The least she could have done was *warn* him.

Actually, it hadn't felt all that bad.

"I had a fun time," Ling continued. "Thank you."

Richard strolled into the enclosure and put his hand on Ryan's shoulder. All three of them silently watched the pandas.

"He's going to make it," Richard said. "But we still have a problem."

"What?" Ryan asked.

"We're going to have to keep Jah-Ni and Chih here for a few months until they recover," Richard replied. "And with things so busy around here, they may not get all the attention they need."

"Can't you hire somebody?"

"I suppose we could . . ." Richard's voice trailed off. Then he cleared his throat and said, "Have any plans for the summer?"

Ryan looked up at his father in shock. "Mean it?"

Richard nodded firmly.

Ryan threw his arms around his dad. If he smiled any harder, he'd pull a muscle.

And he sure didn't want to do that. He needed to be in good health for the long summer.

Behind him, Chih let out a happy bark. One by one, the pandas in the enclosure joined her. The barks rose in a loud chorus. They echoed upward and carried far into the forest, where they were answered again and again, until it seemed that the whole world was shouting with Ryan's joy.